BEASTWALKER

PHARIM WAR BOOK 3

By Gama Ray Martinez

Oracles of Kurnugi
Delphi
Stepmother's Mirror
Mimir's Well

Pharim War
Shadowguard
Veilspeaker
Beastwalker
*Lightbringer**

** Forthcoming*

BEASTWALKER

PHARIM WAR BOOK 3

GAMA RAY MARTINEZ

Cover illustration and desight by Holly Heisey, http://hollyheisey.com

Interior illustrations by Victoria D. Morris

ISBN: 1944091033

ISBN-13: 978-1-944091-03-3

CHAPTER 1

Jez was naked except for the mud. It completely covered him, though a minor effort of will removed it from his hands and face. The excess drained back into the mud pool at his feet. That working wouldn't be enough to get him through this, though. He closed his eyes and concentrated.

Water and earth separated from each other. The water congealed around his torso and arms, and the dirt hardened around his legs. He started to sweat as the water churned, and he drew that sweat into his liquid shirt. He tried to take a step, and the dirt around his legs started to flake away. He focused, hardening the dirt while keeping it flexible enough to move in. He took a breath and stepped over his discarded brown robes. He pulled back the flap to the tent that had been set up to give the challenger a measure of privacy and stepped outside.

Besis, the Academy's protection master, stood there and smiled. He said something, but all of Jez's concentration was being spent on his makeshift clothes. He looked up, and his heart fell. A hundred yards away, trapped by a binding circle of glowing sapphire runes, stood three chezamuts.

The soldier demons, who made up the vast majority of the hordes

of the abyss, were terrible in combat. Facing them would be challenging under ordinary circumstances. He'd done that before, though admittedly with help. Being forced to do it alone while he maintained the earth and water around him would've made dealing with one extremely difficult. Three was beyond impossible. Silently he cursed Besis. The protection master had promised him this would be a fair test, not one that depended on knowledge that had been locked away or on power that would burn away Jez's flesh if he touched it.

As his thoughts raced, the water of his shirt began to drip away, but he caught it before more than a few drops had fallen to the ground. There was nothing left but to try. He started walking toward the circle. After a few seconds, Besis caught up to him. As per tradition, he didn't say anything as he began walking side by side with Jez. They neared the circle, and the red scales of the demons became clear, and the glow of their brass claws became distinct. Their legs were jointed in reverse and ended in cloven hooves. A pair of curved horns rose from their heads, and their eyes were like points of fire.

Jez stopped in front of the circle and took several deep breaths. He glanced up at Besis. The protection master met his gaze. He didn't say anything, but he was sweating and wringing his hands. Jez tried not to look too deeply into that. They were in a small clearing on the slopes of Mount Carcer, and the fire mountain gave off constant heat. That had to be why Besis was sweating. He would never summon creatures for a test that he couldn't handle on his own. Still, Jez hesitated. If he'd been asked a day ago, he would've thought it unlikely that Besis could take on three chezamuts on his own, and certainly not easily enough to defend someone in close quarters. Maybe he'd just underestimated the master.

He looked the chezamuts up and down. A low growl escaped the throat of the one on the right. The other two repeated it a second later. The one on the right tried to slash at him with its claws, but the attack impacted the invisible wall made by the binding circle. The other two did the same as soon as it drew back. They moved at exactly the same time, practically a mirror image of each other. He looked closer. The scales on two of them were a little too smooth. Their movements were jerky, and Jez's eyes wandered to the ground. Only one of the demons left footprints. Understanding dawned on him.

Protection was one of the most demanding dominions, with four schools of magic in addition to more mundane areas of study. Jez had proved his ability with terra and aqua magic by making and maintaining his clothes. Binding would be demonstrated by banishing demons. That only left warding.

It was a struggle to keep the earth and water around him while crafting a third working. The water kept dripping from his hands as they formed patterns in the air, but he let them go. It shouldn't be a problem as long as it wasn't too much. The strain of having to split his concentration three ways made it take longer than it would have otherwise, but finally, a ward against illusion came into being. He felt resistance as it intersected with the binding circle. The wall shimmered but remained intact, and two of the chezamuts vanished. Jez smiled, and out of the corner of his eye, he saw Besis relax. Jez released the ward and started another working. He took a deep breath and stepped into the circle.

Besis cried out, but Jez didn't have time to look. The demon's claws tore through the air at him, and Jez dove to the ground. The earth on his legs cracked and nearly half of it came free. He scrambled to his feet, leaving a wet spot on the ground where his shirt had lost water. The demon lunged at him, trying to catch his arm in its razor sharp teeth. Jez took a step back, and a gout of water shot out from his sleeve and into the demon's face. It backed up several steps. The rest of the earth around Jez legs began to fall away, but he extended the water, melding it with the earth and turning it back into mud. He'd always been more skilled with aqua magic than terra magic.

With the water inside of the earth, he was able to hold the mud in place. He lifted his hand and a beam of silver light shot out. It hit the demon in the chest. The creature roared as the energy of the working drove it back. It tried to take a step forward, but the beam drilled through it, erupting from its back. The fires in its eyes went out. It took one step forward before its skin cracked and silver light shone from within. Its pieces flaked away, turning to ash in the air. In a few moments, the demon was gone.

Jez's shoulders slumped. The mud on his legs began to drip away, and Jez could barely hold on to enough to maintain modesty. Besis clapped.

"Well done, acolyte. Your skill is beyond question."

Jez cocked his head and motioned down at himself. Almost all of his coverings were gone. "But I lost it at the end."

Besis laughed. Jez felt his face heat up. When Besis finally calmed down, he was breathing heavily. "That? You'd be surprised how many people finish this test naked, and it's not just the ones who show as poor judgement as you did."

"What do mean poor judgement?"

Besis cocked an eyebrow. "Stepping into the circle with the chezamut was never a part of this trial. Even master binders don't have to be able to face a soldier demon in single combat."

"But binding..."

"Did it never occur to you to bind it from outside the circle?"

Jez stared at the master for a second and shook his head. "My ward against illusion almost took down the circle. The binding would've destroyed it."

"True, but it still would've gotten the demon."

"But wouldn't that have been cheating?"

Besis raised an eyebrow, and the edges of his mouth tightened in the beginnings of a smile. "Jezreel, I know you've banished more demons than just about anyone, so I would've thought you understood this. There's no such thing as cheating when battling demons." He shook his head. "This is one of the only times someone has entered the circle that I haven't had to step in. Most who succeed not only do it from outside the circle, they do it from a great distance. Granted, their first attempt usually hits an illusion, but they still have time to craft another working before the chezamut reaches them."

Jez nodded. "I didn't even think of that."

"Well, you've had more direct contact with demons than anyone else I've ever trained. Still, you should try to remember that a direct assault isn't always the best choice."

Jez inclined his head. "Yes, Master Besis."

Besis waved at the tent. "Now put on your robes. The ceremony will begin at sunset. Well done."

Jez bowed his head to the master and couldn't stop grinning. It felt like a lifetime ago that he'd come to the Academy, though in fact, it had only been a year. He'd changed so much since then, and today, he would take a major step forward. He ducked into the tent and put on his acolyte robes for the last time. At the Ceremony of Raising, he, along with the rest who had proven themselves ready, would be given the colored robes of an adept.

CHAPTER 2

The Ceremony of Raising took place in the courtyard near the center of the Academy. The central spire rose two hundred feet above them and loomed like some great beast. The obsidian that covered most of the city shimmered in the light of the setting sun. Students and family members were gathered to honor those who would be promoted. Jez could see the tall form of Osmund in the crowd.

The giant of a boy had already been at the Academy several terms when Jez had arrived and had received his own adept's robes two terms ago. Now, the scarlet garment of a destruction adept seemed almost like flames in the setting sun. Lina stood next to him, seeming tiny by comparison, though she was of average height. Her blond hair gleamed in the sunlight. She had only returned to the Academy three terms ago, but she had been promoted the previous term. She hadn't stopped lording over Jez that she'd been declared an adept before he had, but it had been a friendly sort of teasing, unlike the cruel attitude she'd held in her first term.

Jez stood with five other brown-robed students before the stairs leading to the tower. Only the dominion of beasts was unrepresented, which was odd because Jez knew a boy named Barash had been set to test for promotion in that dominion. The door to the tower opened and Chancellor Balud, master of healing and head of the Carceri Academy, walked forward and stopped at the top of the stairs. Three masters, including Besis, appeared on his left, and two came to his right. Master Horgar, master of beasts, was missing. The crowd started whispering. Even though Horgar didn't have an acolyte being raised, it was tradition for all seven masters to take part in the ceremony. Balud stepped forward.

"When Lenur, first king of Ashtar established this kingdom, he recognized that there were matters beyond the influence of any king. He decreed that a group of men and women establish a school to teach people to deal with things outside the purview of ordinary law, and thus the Carceri Academy was born.

"Those who leave this place as mages have a responsibility to the people, be they of Ashtar or of any other land, but the road to magehood is long, and few can see it through to its end. You six have taken the first step. Acolytes, you have all demonstrated your knowledge and ability in your chosen dominion. As such, it is no longer fitting to call you acolytes. You are adepts of the Carceri Academy. Let your respective masters come forth and present you with the robes of your office."

Balud stepped forward and held out an orange robe to a petite girl named Michena. She beamed as she took it, and her eyes went wide as the chancellor inclined his head. One by one, the others presented their robes. Master Linala had yellow, Rael had indigo. Kerag's was violet and Fina's was red. Besis walked up to Jez and held out a brilliant blue robe. He took it and realized his hands were shaking. He'd been at the Academy for six terms, a full year, not counting the time he'd spent at the capital, working toward this goal. Now, it was hard to believe it was actually happening. He inclined his head, but

Besis bowed deeply to him. From the way the other masters looked at him, it was clear this wasn't normal.

"Well earned, Jezreel Bartinson. Well earned."

The other former acolytes were engaged in short conversation with their masters, and Jez was about to do the same when a shadow fell over the gathered people. Everyone looked up at the massive bird descending on the courtyard. It had dark brown feathers and was large enough that it could carry a person in each of its talons. Its curved beak looked well suited to tearing at flesh, and Jez couldn't help but wonder what this creature ate. A few started screaming and some of Fina's students raised their hands and prepared to fling balls of fire.

"Extinguish," the destruction master called.

His voice bellowed over the noise of the people, and instantly the fires went out, leaving only the faint smell of smoke hanging in the air. The burly man held his hands clasped together in front of him. When he spread them out, a blast of wind shot into the crowd, forcing them apart and giving the bird a place to land. Jez hadn't noticed the pair of smaller birds latched on to the wings of the larger creature.

They looked like miniature versions of the massive hawk, and as soon as it landed, they detached themselves and perched next to their larger counterpart. All three shimmered. For a moment, the larger hawk shrank, but it grew back to normal size a second later. It closed its eyes and gave the peculiar impression that it was concentrating, and all three of the birds shimmered and vanished, revealing three green robed figures. The larger hawk had been Master Horgar. In his hands, he held the unmoving form of Barash, the one who was to have been tested for promotion into the dominion of beasts. The black veil on his face spoke louder than any words anyone could've said. Barash was dead.

CHAPTER 3

Everyone started shouting at once. A man and a woman Jez didn't recognize rushed past him, probably Barash's mother and father. They knelt by the body, and the woman started weeping. Master Horgar spoke softly to them. Jez took a deep breath, sniffing at the air and almost immediately calmed a little. Balud raised a hand toward the crowd, but no one seemed to be paying attention. He glanced over at Master Kerag. The large man nodded, and when Balud spoke, his voice came out like a thunderclap.

"Silence!"

Even the wind seemed to die down at his command. Every eye, save those of the dead student's parents, turned to the chancellor, and he lowered his hands.

"You will all disperse. Students are free from obligation until the next term begins. Masters will come to my office. Go."

The crowd looked at one another, but Balud cleared his throat. Still enhanced by Kerag's audio illusion, it sounded like the rumble of the earth, and the people scattered slowly. Balud called a few of his adjutants to come and prepare the body and care for the parents. Jez made his way through the crowd. It didn't take him long to find Osmund. People actually parted around the large boy. Lina was standing next to him. The two, while not exactly friends, were no longer the bitter enemies they had been once.

"Did you smell...anything?" Osmund asked.

Jez glanced around, but no one seemed to be paying attention. Still, he didn't want to answer Osmund's unspoken question out loud, so he just shook his head. Lina let out a breath in obvious relief. The motion seemed to accentuate the scar on her face. The mark, made by the sword of Osmund's alter ego, Ziary, couldn't be healed by magic or nature. Once, she'd used an illusion to hide it, but after getting caught up in a plot to unleash a demon general, such things had ceased to matter very much for her, and she'd put away that particular conceit. She noticed him looking and gave him a half smile. Jez nodded and led them down an alley before he elaborated further.

"It's probably nothing," Jez said. Then he winced at his own words. Barash had been a quiet and mild mannered boy. Jez had liked him. A lot of people had. "I mean it's not nothing. It probably wasn't demons. These trials can be dangerous. Just because the masters haven't lost anyone in a long time doesn't mean it can't happen."

Absently, Osmund rubbed his right forearm. After his own trial, that arm had been badly burned. Lina nodded, no doubt remembering the nightmares that had plagued her until well into the term. The masters didn't allow anyone to go through a trial until they were ready, but there were no guarantees. Maybe Barash had made a mistake as bad as Jez himself had, only without being so lucky. That was probably it.

They went to the Quarter Horse, one of the town's inns, where they were joined by a blue-robed boy named Kilos, who was the son of the innkeeper. Jez had saved his life from a fear demon the previous year. Their plan had been to celebrate Jez's promotion, but with the death of Barash, the mood of their dinner was muted.

After a little while, a woman with raven hair started playing the flute. Jez tried to get into the music, but he just kept seeing Barash's face. The others seemed to share his feelings, and after only an hour, he called over Lufka. The innkeeper refused payment, and Jez tried to insist. It was an old argument, one that they'd been having ever since Jez saved his son's life. Normally Jez won, but this time, his heart wasn't in it, and he thanked Lufka for the meal and got up to leave. His friends tried to convince him to stay a little while longer, but he could tell they would be as happy as he would when this night was done.

He was halfway back to the tower when he realized what was bothering him. The Academy was supposed to be safe. There were wards and safeguards spread throughout the city, and there were even more in the Academy grounds itself. People got hurt sometimes, of course. The wards did nothing to protect against ordinary harm. Every once in a while, a rogue demon would escape from the summoner or a pyromage would lose control of a particularly volatile working, but it was never anything serious. Even the demon lord Marrowit had had his physical form destroyed when he'd attacked the Academy. Death simply had no place here. The fact that Barash had obviously been killed elsewhere seemed not to matter. This place had become home in the past year, and it shouldn't have happened. Intellectually, he knew the sentiment didn't make sense. Still, he couldn't shake the thought as he entered the tower.

The building was unusually silent for so early in the evening, and he climbed to his quarters without seeing anyone. He pushed open the door and didn't bother to light the lantern before falling into bed. The light of the full moon shone through the window, and Jez found himself staring at it, reflecting on the events of the past year. He practically jumped out of his skin when someone stepped between him and the window.

He rolled to his feet and called water out of the air, shrouding his right hand in it and imbuing the liquid with power. The water took on a blue glow and illuminated a man with tanned skin and eyes bluer than anything Jez had ever seen. His sapphire robes seemed to shimmer with their own inner light. The water at Jez's hand splashed to the ground, and he almost bowed before he remembered this being wouldn't appreciate the gesture.

"Well, you certainly are jumpy."

His voice was soft, and some of Jez's anxiousness drained away. He flicked his hand toward the lantern, and it sputtered to life. The amount of effort it took made him wish he'd used flint and steel instead, but he'd been too surprised to take his limited ability with fire into consideration.

The light illuminated a face that had seen more ages than a mortal mind could comprehend.

"Hello Sariel."

One of the most powerful beings in existence inclined his head. "Luntayary."

CHAPTER 4

The seven pharim lords had presided over the creation of the universe itself. Their power was beyond anything humankind could imagine. Each had an army of lesser pharim under their command. Together, they watched over reality, only interfering when mortals meddled in matters best left alone. The secret known to few was that the pharim Luntayary had been cursed by the mage Dusan, bound to human flesh for one lifetime. He had been born as a human child, as Jez. Luntayary was a Shadowguard, a protector and a guardian, and Sariel was the pharim lord over all the Shadowguards.

"My name is Jezreel," Jez said. "I don't remember being Luntayary."

Sariel inclined his head. "Fair point, and it is with Jezreel that I wish to speak. This is a matter that requires mortal choice."

Jez nodded. As powerful as they were, pharim were bound by strict rules that they could not violate. One of the most important was that they could not violate mortal choice. As a human, however, Jez was free to ignore that restriction, and at great personal risk, he could still draw on Luntayary's power. That gave him options not open to most people, and he'd been forced to use that power a couple of times.

"What do you need?"

"You saw the dead student that the master of beasts brought."

Jez nodded. "I didn't think he was killed by a demon."

"He wasn't. An animal killed him, an ordinary beast of the field. It wasn't even rabid."

Jez blinked. "But Barash studied beasts. He should've been able to handle an ordinary animal."

"He would've been if his magic had not failed."

Jez pursed his lips and thought back to when the beast master had changed forms. Sariel's face was completely still in the lantern light as Jez gathered his thoughts. "Master Horgar had trouble transforming. I thought I was imagining it."

"All beast magic will fail, given time."

"Why?"

"Aniel is missing."

For a second, Jez just stared. Sariel met his gaze without blinking. Jez wondered if he was making some sort of cosmic joke. He shook his head. The very idea of a high lord of the pharim joking might have made him laugh if the situation wasn't so serious.

"Aniel is missing?"

"Yes, as I said."

Jez shook his head, sure he was misunderstanding. "What do you mean missing?"

Sariel rolled his eyes. Jez hadn't known a pharim lord would do that. "It's not a difficult word. You know exactly what it means. He is gone. He cannot be located. None of the Beastwalkers can be."

"None of them?"

"None."

"Where did Aniel go?"

"I do not know. No one does. If we did, he would not be missing."

"But can't you find him?"

"Obviously not. That's why I came to you."

"I don't know where he is."

"I didn't think that you did, but you can find him."

Jez gaped at him. He had no idea how to respond, and in the end, he just spouted the first thing that came to mind. "How?"

"I don't know."

"Then why do you think I can find him?"

"Perhaps it would be more accurate to say that we can't find him."

"But you're..." Jez didn't know how to finish his sentence so he just gestured at Sariel.

"Exactly."

Jez took several deep breaths trying to make sense of everything, but his mind was racing. "I don't understand."

"We were created with a specific purpose, and we can step outside of that only loosely. There is no pharim who can interfere in Aniel's affairs."

"And I can?"

"You are mortal. You can choose."

"But he's missing. If you find him, that's not interfering."

"And if he doesn't wish to be found?"

That made Jez pause. "You think he's hiding?"

"Even his essence has vanished from the Keep of the Hosts." Sariel let out a long breath, and the gesture made chills run down Jez's spine. "He is hiding or he is held. I do not know which is more likely, nor do I know which scares me more."

So many thoughts were racing through his head. Jez didn't know where to begin. Finally, he just sighed.

"What do you want me to do?"

"I can only offer you limited advice. Normally, beast magic would be strong near Aniel, but that's only if he's free. If he's been bound, somehow, beast magic might be disrupted, and those disturbances would center on him."

"So look for places where beast magic is stronger than it should be or places where it's weaker?"

"It's an imperfect solution. More than any other school, beast magic wanes and waxes, but it's the best idea I can give you."

"I'll do what I can," Jez said.

"Thank you."

He started to fade, but Jez called out.

"Sariel."

"Yes?" his disembodied voice said.

"Could he have been destroyed?"

Silence stretched out for several long seconds, and Jez wondered if Sariel had gone.

"If Aniel has been destroyed," the voice said finally, "may the Creator help us all."

He sounded afraid, and that, more than anything else, terrified Jez. It didn't make sense for Aniel to hide, but the Lord of the Beastwalkers was one of the high lords of the pharim. What in all of creation could hold one of the most powerful beings in existence?

CHAPTER 5

Jez paced back and forth in his room for nearly an hour trying to think of what to do. He needed to talk to the masters about Barash, but they wouldn't lightly discuss the death with a student, and he would have to think of a convincing reason to get them to do so. Telling them that Sariel had appeared in his room, and had told him to find a missing pharim lord, was more likely to make them think his mind had cracked than to get any sensitive information out of them. In the end, he decided to go see Besis. The protection master was one of the handful of people who knew Jez had been a pharim. He reached for the door but before he touched it, a loud crash came from the other side, shaking his room. Screaming erupted from the hall outside.

Again, he drew water out of the air and shrouded his hand in it. Then, he pulled open the door and froze. Four students, three of them mere acolytes, huddled at the other end of the hall. Between Jez and them stood a bull larger than any Jez had ever seen. At least eight feet tall, it would've towered over even Osmund. Its body was almost as wide as the passage itself. Its fur seemed black though in the dim light of the hall, it was impossible to be sure. Muscles rippled as it pawed at the ground, the motion cracking the stones beneath its hooves. It lowered its head and charged.

One of the students, a blue robed girl name Liandra lifted a hand. The ground groaned and a wall of stone appeared in between the students and the bull. The animal crashed into it, shattering the stone and shaking the ground. A few doors opened, and students poked their heads out, but as soon as they saw the bull, they retreated. The bull didn't notice. It kept its eyes locked on the cowering students.

They were covered in dust. Liandra tried to call up another wall, but the bull stomped, shaking the ground and kicking up rock dust. Liandra sneezed, losing her grip on the working. An acolyte Jez didn't know raised a hand. A ball of fire appeared but puffed out of existence a second later. The student closed his eyes and tried to concentrate, but he was obviously too afraid.

"Toden!" someone cried out.

A girl in a green robe ran out of a shattered hole in the wall and started running toward the animal. The bull snorted and looked back at her. For a second, Jez thought it would charge her, though he couldn't imagine how it would turn around. After a few moments, however, it returned its attention to the four before it.

"That thing is a student?" Jez cried out.

The girl glanced at him and nodded. The bull lifted its hooves, but Liandra threw her hands forward and a piece of shattered wall as big as her head flew at the bull. The animal slammed its hooves into the stone. The blow reduced the rock to dust, and its hoof crashed into Liandra's head. She went down, blood running down the side of her face, but the rock had apparently taken enough of the force behind the blow because almost immediately, she started to stand again.

Jez threw his hands forward, pulling water from anywhere he could find. He drew it from the stone and the air. The people provided a source too, though he was careful not to draw too deeply

from them. He even reached into the bull itself. Tendrils materialized and lashed onto the animal. It strained, and Jez could feel its strength as it struggled against his constructs. His skin felt dry, and the air parched his throat. The bull groaned and slammed his head against the wall, snapping off the tip of its left horn. Then, it fell to the ground, held by bands of water stronger than steel.

The girl looked at Jez and nodded. Slowly, she went up to the bull and closed her eyes. Green light emerged from her hands as she held them against the bull's side, but after a few seconds she sighed.

"I can't change him back."

"Get Master Horgar," Jez said through clenched teeth.

He would've been sweating if he hadn't used so much water from his own body to form the bands. The creature was just so strong, and Jez held himself on the cusp of tapping Luntayary's power. The girl nodded and disappeared through the door leading to the stairway that ran around the inner wall of the tower.

Liandra hadn't been able to stand but had managed to sit. She blinked several times and stared at the bull. Suddenly, her eyes went wide as if seeing it for the first time. She raised her hands and the bull sank into the stone a few inches. It struggled against it, but with Liandra's earth working taking some of the pressure off of Jez, he could hold the creature much more easily. Rocks began to crawl up its body, partially encasing it in stone. The pressure against Jez's bindings lessened even more. The three acolytes with her helped her to her feet and she staggered to Jez.

"The people on the floor beneath us are getting an entertaining view," she said as she wiped away some of the blood on her face. She seemed to have trouble focusing.

"Won't it fall through?"

"Eventually. It would've gotten free if I hadn't done anything."

She inclined her head to him. "I'm impressed. I didn't realize you were strong enough to hold something like that with water."

"Neither did I."

By then, other advanced students had arrived, and the bull was thoroughly tied up with various sorts of magic. Jez released his own bonds, and his arms suddenly felt very heavy. The working had drained him, and he had to lean on a wall to remain standing. One of Balud's adjutants made the bull sleep, and several others who specialized in terra magic lifted it out of Liandra's trap and laid it on the ground. Balud's student was seeing to Liandra when Horgar arrived. The beast master wasted no time in attending to the bull. An aura of green light appeared around the animal. It shimmered for a second but otherwise remained unchanged. Horgar looked over his shoulder at the student who had brought him.

"Lacia, three horns."

She nodded and closed her eyes. Horgar did the same. He opened his eyes a second later, and the light around the bull intensified. Slowly, the bull began to shrink under the master's hand. It took a few minutes for the image of a sandy haired boy, only a few years older than Jez himself, to appear. Horgar lifted his unconscious form and placed him gently on the floor.

CHAPTER 6

It wasn't long before the other masters arrived. With Balud directing his students, the injured were soon seen to. Liandra had a head injury that might've been dangerous if not for the workings of the healers, which stopped the bleeding and closed the wound. The chancellor ordered Liandra to be brought to the healing house, and the rest he sent to their rooms.

"You, and you," Horgar said pointing to Jez and one of the acolytes who had come out to see what was going on. "Put Toden on a stretcher and carry him to my quarters. I will see to him."

"He really should go to the healing house," Balud said.

Horgar shook his head. "We've both seen this before. There's nothing wrong with his body, and you know it." The beast master clucked his tongue and turned to a female master in an indigo robe. "Rael, if you would come with me, I could use your help."

The secrets master nodded. "Of course."

In short order, they had carried Toden to Master Horgar's house in the beast district. The beast master's home was a single story building that took up half a block. Stables attached to it housed some of the largest horses Jez had ever seen. There was even one with black and white stripes. Jez had no idea where Horgar had found that creature. A nest of crows sat over the front door, and the birds cawed as they passed under the nest. The inside of the building held cages of birds and small rodents. They all started calling when the party entered but they went quiet at a wave of Horgar's hand.

"Put him in here," Horgar said.

He walked into a hall and pushed open a door. The room inside was plain, and had nothing more than a bed and a small table. Jez and the acolyte put Toden on the bed and exchange glances. Rael put a hand on the unconscious student's forehead. Jez expected to be ordered to leave, but Horgar just walked out. He came back a few seconds later holding a green crystal, no larger than a thumbnail, that hung from a gold chain. Jez stared at it. Focusing crystals were extremely rare and valuable artifacts. Even the masters didn't know how they had been made. The crystals didn't strengthen magic so much as they concentrated it and granted a greater degree of control, allowing a person to do more with the same amount of power. This one was attuned to beast magic, and it started glowing as Horgar held it over Toden. After a few seconds, Horgar let out a breath and looked at the secrets master.

"It's no use. I can't retrieve him. Can you do anything?"

"Beast mind?" Rael asked. Horgar nodded and the secrets master shook her head. "It's been tried before. It doesn't work."

"This is no ordinary beast mind. He's a skilled adjutant, and he was lucid this afternoon."

"That's not possible."

"But yet it happened."

"What happened?" Jez asked.

The two masters looked at him, each wearing a surprised expression. Jez found himself wishing he hadn't spoken.

"You shouldn't be eavesdropping adept," Horgar said.

Rael laughed. "You can hardly call it eavesdropping if we simply forgot they were here, but Master Horgar is right. This is no place for you."

The acolyte bowed and scurried out of the room. Jez looked at Toden. "But..."

"Go, Jezreel."

The tone in her voice did not allow for argument. Jez inclined his head and left, but he sat against the wall of the house for a long time. He was so distracted by everything that had happened that he didn't even notice Osmund and Lina next to him until Osmund tapped him on the shoulder.

"This is bad, isn't it?" Lina asked.

Jez just nodded.

"As bad as Sharim or Dusan?" Osmund asked.

Jez looked from one to the other. Dusan had summoned a nightmare demon that had threatened to put the entire world into a slumber so it could feed off their fears. Sharim had nearly toppled the kingdom, but this could be a disaster on an entirely different level. Briefly, he considered not telling them, but they had been through too much together. He nodded.

"I think it might be worse than both of them put together. Come on. Let's go somewhere we can talk privately. I'll tell you everything."

CHAPTER 7

A pharim lord was in your room?" Lina asked for the third time.

"Yes," Jez said. "Can we please move past that?"

"This room right here?"

"Yes. He was standing right over there."

"Sariel himself?"

"You saw a pharim at Rumar," Jez pointed out. "Why is this so much harder to believe?"

She banged her hands on the table in frustration. "Yes, but...Sariel."

"He's actually pretty nice."

The flickering lantern light combined with the moonlight streaming through the window made Osmund's grin look wicked. Lina's jaw dropped, and she gaped at him for a second before turning to Jez who nodded.

"Osmund met him last year when we were dealing with the sleeping sickness."

"Sariel?"

Osmund let out a breath, and though he did an excellent job of hiding his smile, Jez could hear the laughter in his voice. "I think you broke her."

That snapped her out of it, and she turned to glare at the giant boy. "Maybe I'm just surprised he would show himself to a freak like you."

Once, those words would've angered Osmund, but then, once Lina would've actually meant them. Instead Osmund just laughed, and Lina blushed.

"Sorry," she said. "This is all just so much."

"Do either of you know what beast mind is?" Jez asked.

Lina nodded. "When someone changes forms, they gain the instincts of a beast. Students aren't allowed to even attempt it until Master Horgar is convinced their will is strong enough to avoid being overpowered by it. Otherwise, the instincts would take control. If that happened even changing back to human form wouldn't help."

"Why did Rael think it was impossible?" Jez asked.

Osmund raised an eyebrow. "And how do you know so much about beasts?"

"I know about the mind," Lina said. "Master Rael says I have a gift."

"Why did she think it was impossible for Toden to have a beast mind?" Jez asked again.

"Because Toden is an adjutant. He knows what he's doing. An adjutant of beasts would have to be transformed for weeks or months before something like this happened. It can't happen in a single day. It would be like Osmund losing a fight to a farmer armed with a stick. It's just not going to happen."

"Do you think Aniel is somewhere nearby?" Osmund asked.

Jez shrugged. "I don't know. Sariel said the disruptions would be happening everywhere. They just might be more concentrated wherever Aniel is. Maybe if it happened again, but I don't think this tells us anything for sure."

All three of them jumped when someone started banging on the door. Jez got up and answered it. Kosor, the adjutant of knowledge who had been raised earlier that day, stood on the outside. The stout boy looked from Jez to Osmund and Lina.

"It's happened again," he said.

"What has?"

Kosor absently waved his hand behind him at where the bull had attacked, though the damage to the tower had already been repaired. "A student transformed into a wolf in the middle of town." For a second, he looked like he was going to be sick. "Three people were killed before she was restrained."

"Killed?"

Kosor nodded. "Besis sent me to find you. He wants to see you right away."

Jez nodded. "I'm on my way."

Kosor nodded and ran off. Jez and his friends walked out of his room, but before they parted ways, Osmund grabbed his arm.

"So do you think Aniel is nearby?"

Jez was about to nod, but paused. It just didn't feel right. He shrugged. "I don't know."

CHAPTER 8

The protection master's home was the same size as Horgar's, though it was decorated completely differently. A massive fountain stood in front, and symbols of protection had been carved into the walls. Jez lifted his hand to knock, but the door swung inward before he got a chance. Besis stood on the other side.

"Jezreel, good. Please, come in."

Shields from different noble houses hung from the walls, and Jez instinctively sought out the closed fist that had belonged to Dusan. It hung right next to the blue starfish that Jez had taken for his own sigil. At some point in the past year, Besis had acquired half a dozen suites of armor that stood neatly at one end of his receiving room. He motioned for Jez to sit on a cushioned chair near the fireplace. Besis took a seat next to him.

"What do you think?" he asked.

"About what?"

"About this madness."

Jez blinked at him and spoke slowly, trying to figure out what the master was getting at. "I don't know sir. I'm not a healer."

"Is it like the sleeping sickness?"

"Sir?"

Besis let out a breath and leaned forward in his chair. "By the time we knew the sleeping sickness was being used to feed power into Dusan's ritual, it had already spread too far to stop. Maybe if we had caught it early, we could've prevented a great deal of suffering. I don't want to make the same mistake twice. You helped carry one of the inflicted earlier today. Was it caused by demonic power like the sleeping sickness?"

"Master Besis, I didn't even think to look for that." Jez bit his lower lip and shook his head. "No, I don't think so. That's not something I would've missed."

Besis sighed. "I don't know if I should be happy that it's not what we're dealing with or upset because we're still no closer to finding out what is the matter."

Jez pursed his lips. "I may know something."

"Oh?"

"Sariel came to me earlier. I was on my way to tell you when Toden attacked."

It only took a few minutes to explain. Besis, for his part, was more ready to accept his story than Lina had been. When he was done, Besis let out a breath.

"This is even worse than I thought. A high lord of the pharim, missing."

"What happened to Barash?" Jez asked.

Besis blinked at him. "He died."

"I know, but why?"

Besis let out a breath. "Horgar said he ran into a family of apes. They were more hostile than they normally are, but Toden still should've been able to handle that. He didn't though. He didn't even transform, though he apparently tried to do something. Whatever it was didn't work though and the apes beat him. Before Horgar could interfere, they had collapsed his chest."

"I thought Horgar could calm animals from a long way away."

Besis shrugged. "Normally he can, but it's not a precise magic, especially if a creature is feeling a strong emotion or is diseased. Distance weakens it too."

Jez nodded. "So maybe that's what Barash was trying to do, and the animals were too angry to respond."

Besis raised an eyebrow. "Would you fail to banish an imp from a few inches away?"

Jez snorted. Imps were such minor spiritual beings that, on occasion, they had been banished by housewives with wooden paddles. Jez could deal with one without breaking a sweat. Besis grunted.

"Where are you going to look for Aniel?"

Jez glanced out of Besis's window. It faced the center of the city, and Jez could barely make out the central spire. He turned back and met the master's gaze.

"There have been two incidents here. It only makes sense to start with the basement of the tower."

"You can't go into the lower levels without special permission." Jez shrugged, and Besis rolled his eyes. "Why there?"

"There are wards on the lower levels, and they were put there with the power of an erupting fire mountain. I can't think of any other place that has even a chance of holding Aniel. We might have had more than just the two incidents, if I'm right about Horgar struggling to transform."

Besis frowned. "You noticed that, did you?"

Jez shook his head. "Not right away. After Sariel left, I thought about it and realized what I'd seen. That's probably why he had to use a contingent to restore Toden."

Besis stared at him for a second before chuckling. "You seem to have unraveled all of Horgar's secrets. I'll take you to the lower levels, but I doubt you'll find a trapped pharim lord there."

"Do you have a better idea?"

"Grinta, the student who turned into a wolf, was one of those who came back with Horgar. Barash's magic failed him when he was doing his trial, and Horgar was there too. Aniel could be at their training ground. We can speak to Horgar. He may have more information."

Jez nodded. "I've been trying to think of way to get him to talk to me."

"I'll take care of it. It'll have to wait until after the trial though."

"What trial?"

Besis raised an eyebrow. "A student used transformation magic to kill three people. We can't just ignore that. Grinta has to be tried. I'm afraid there's little doubt she'll be found guilty and most likely, sentenced to death."

CHAPTER 9

Jez sat with Osmund and Lina among a dozen others as Grita, her hands tied together, was led into the large house in the district of shadows. Her coarse black hair stuck out in every direction, and her eyes looked wild. She bared her teeth at the gathered crowd. Another rope bound her feet, though there was enough slack on that one to allow her to walk. It didn't do any good. She tried to run, but she tripped and slammed into the ground. The violet robed adept moved to help her up, but Grita snarled at him and he drew back. He looked up at Master Kerag who was seated with the other masters at a long table at one end of the room. The shadows master sighed and glanced at Rael who was seated next him. She waved a hand at Grita and the student calmed. She stood up with her eyes half closed and shambled forward listlessly until she'd reached the center of the room. Balud narrowed his eyes.

"We need her able to answer questions not be asleep on her feet."

Rael shook her head. "Her mind is gone. It's been shattered so completely by the wolf that it may as well not be there. This trial is pointless."

"It isn't," Horgar said. Rael glared at him, and he raised a hand. He looked like he hated himself for what he was about to say. "We cannot allow a mad mage to roam the world, and you cannot cage a wild animal without consigning it to a slow death. I will not permit that for one of mine, and I will not pass sentence on a mage such as her without a trial."

"She's sick, Horgar, not a killer."

"She's both, and she's extremely dangerous."

"But…"

"My lords?" It was a soft, squeaky voice that spoke. A stout man whose hair had been reduced to a few tufts of grey stepped out of the crowd. He was wringing his hands, and took Jez a second to recognize Mishor, the mayor of Tarcai. "We depend on you to protect us from things like that." He pointed at Grita, seeming not to notice the nearly universal glares the students were giving him. He had just unwittingly insulted every mage in the room. "If you're not going to do that, please tell us now, and I'll arrange for an evacuation."

"Calm yourself, Goodman Mishor," Besis said as he waved his hand to placate the mayor. "I assure you, we will deal with this matter appropriately. Now, please sit."

They mayor sat down next to the families of Grita's victims. He muttered something Jez couldn't hear to the woman sitting next to him as Grita was led to a chair in front of the masters. She stared blankly up at them. Kerag glanced to Balud who shrugged and nodded.

"Grita Anendatter, you are accused of the murder of Aownen Hakendatter, Odar Sakerson, and Brenon Kasison. What do you say to this?" She just stared at him blankly. Kerag turned to Rael. "Restore her, please."

"It won't do any good."

"I can't put a person one trial while they're under the influence of

mental magic and have it be fair."

"It won't be fair regardless," Rael said.

"Do it," Balud said.

"But chancellor," she began.

"I don't like it any more than you do. Let's get this over with as soon as we can."

She scowled but nodded. She raised a hand. Almost instantly, Grita raised her head and howled. The sound sent shivers running down Jez's spine, and many of the gathered people twitched in their seats. More than one threw a glance at the door. When the howl faded, the room was completely silent. The mayor and those with him looked ready to run. Most of the students were doing better, though some weren't by much. Grita leapt forward, but she was still in the air when Fina waved at her and a gust of wind forced her back down. The destruction master stood.

"This is ridiculous. She's little more than an animal. Horgar, can you take care of this?"

"What do you mean take care of it? I'm not going to put her down, if that's what you mean."

"This is your dominion. Do with her as you will."

"The mage law," Balud started.

Fina made a slashing motion with his hand. "By any reasonable standard, that girl is no mage. If her mind is restored, we can try her. If not...you don't punish a wolf for being a wolf."

"He's right," Rael said.

One by one, the other masters nodded until only Balud was left. The chancellor looked from the masters to the families of the victims. Finally, he nodded.

"Grita is a wild animal. As such, what happens to her is rightfully under the jurisdiction of Master Horgar. If she is ever seen in the city with her mind restored, she will be tried. Until such a day, the matter is closed." The mayor stood up and started to speak, but he went silent at Balud's glare. "What would you have me do? Look at her."

The mayor kept his eyes on Balud for almost a full minute. Behind him, some of the people glanced at the bound girl, but most avoided looking in her direction. A woman with dark skin and hair shook her head and walked out without saying a word. As if her departure had opened the floodgates, people started trickling away until only the mayor was left. He closed his eyes and lowered his head. He walked out without saying a word, and Jez let out a breath he hadn't realized he was holding.

CHAPTER 10

People trickled out of the trial room until the only ones aside from the masters were Jez, Osmund, and Lina. Balud looked at Jez in the eye and opened his mouth to speak but Besis touched his arm and shook his head. Balud nodded, but Jez told his friends to go. Osmund looked like he was going to argue, but when he saw the look on Jez's face, he inclined his head. Lina looked between the two of them and nodded. The pair left without saying a word. Jez turned back to walk up toward the platform of the masters but was surprised when he saw Horgar heading right toward him.

"Besis said you wished to speak with me. Do you know what's going on with beast magic?"

Jez looked nervously at the other masters. None, aside from Besis, seemed to be paying attention, but he still hesitated to speak. Horgar glanced over his shoulder and nodded. He motioned for Jez to follow. Lina and Osmund were waiting outside. They moved to come after them but stopped at a shake of Jez's head. After a short walk, Jez and Horgar arrived at a small building in the beasts district. Horgar pushed open the door. It was full of sacks of grain and seed. To Jez's surprise, the beast master plopped down on one, releasing a cloud of grain dust, and a faint sweet smell reached Jez's nose. The masters had always seemed regal and noble to him, but Master Horgar looked perfectly natural sitting on a sack of grain, and the sight made Jez smile, but he stopped when Horgar met his eyes.

"Now, tell me what is the matter."

For a second, Jez was unsure about how to start. "Have you ever met Aniel?" he asked eventually.

Horgar let out a sharp breath and inclined his head slightly in what Jez suspected was an unconscious motion. "The lord of beasts himself? No, I've never had the honor, not him nor any who serve him. Why?"

Jez bit his lower lip and tried to think of the best way to say it. Finally, he just let it out.

"Because he's missing."

"Who's missing?"

"Aniel."

Horgar stared at him for a few moments before speaking. "Jezreel, this is no time for jokes." He stopped speaking when he saw the expression on Jez's face, and he paled a little. "You're serious, aren't you?" Jez nodded. "Is this another one of those pieces of knowledge that rises up from your scion?"

Jez nodded and hoped Horgar didn't see the lie on his face. Aside from Besis and a handful of others, everyone believed that Jez's power and flashes of insight were the result of him being a limaph, a person descended from the pharim. Some limaph, such as Osmund, could transform into a being akin to a pharim, though nowhere near as powerful. Occasionally, limaph knew things they had no way of knowing, and it was a convenient story Jez had occasionally used. Horgar nodded.

"Besis speaks highly of you as does Rael, and your word carries a lot of weight with them, especially in matters concerning the pharim.

Otherwise, I would think you were making up stories."

"You believe me?"

Horgar sighed and placed his hand on the sack he was sitting on. A spider climbed onto his finger, and he lifted it in front of his face. He stared at it for several seconds as it crawled up his finger. When it reached his wrist, he allowed it to crawl back onto the grain sack. He shook his head.

"I wish I didn't. Two people have suffered beast mind when that should've been impossible. I can't think of anything that would cause it, but a missing pharim lord? Who knows what effects that could have?"

"Transformation is failing, isn't it?"

Horgar sighed, and Jez thought he wasn't going to answer, but after a few seconds, the beasts master nodded. "I can't tell for sure when it started happening. Thinking back, there were a thousand tiny signs that I dismissed. I never should've taken Barash to be tested." He managed a weak smile. "That's how it is, isn't it? We look back at all the decisions we should have made, as if we could've known better then. I'm sorry. I'm rambling. Yes, transformation is failing, as is the magic we use to talk to beasts."

"Aniel's presence would disrupt or enhance beast magic. With people getting beast mind and with you having trouble..." Horgar glanced at him with raised eyebrow and Jez cleared his throat. "With everything else that's been going on around here, I thought he might be imprisoned under the tower, but Besis said you might have other ideas."

Horgar rose and walked to the small window. He looked out and didn't say anything. There were a few spots of grain dust on his robe, but Horgar seemed not to notice. Seconds stretched to minutes, and Jez wondered if he should say something. Finally, Horgar turned around.

"I suspect Besis is right. I doubt someone could imprison a high lord of the pharim under the tower without us knowing. You should still check just to be sure."

"Where do you think he could be?"

Horgar shook his head. "I'll handle it."

"But..."

The master lifted a hand to silence Jez. "I know you've dealt with difficult situations before, but you were thrust into those and had no chance to avoid them. I'm not about to deliberately send you into something like this. You are only an adept, and a new one at that. I'm not going to force you into a situation properly handled by a master."

"I can—"

"I'm sure you can, but I'm not going to send a child into something like this. Thank you for the information. I'll see to it this matter is dealt with."

"But, Master..."

"I'll handle it, Jezreel. Check the rooms beneath the tower. I'll take care of the rest."

Horgar stared down at him. It was clearly a dismissal. Jez considered arguing, but the look on the master's face told him it would do no good. He nodded and walked out of the grain house. Just before the door closed behind him, he looked over his shoulder at Horgar who was once again looking through the window. Jez just hoped the master knew what he was doing.

CHAPTER 11

Y ou have to admit," Osmund said, "It makes sense."

"I know it makes sense," Jez said. "It's also wrong."

Lina drummed her fingers on Jez's table. They were in Jez's room. Lina and Osmund had been waiting at his door when he had gotten back. He'd invited them in and told them about his meeting with Horgar.

"Jez, are you sure that you're not too sure of yourself?" Lina asked. "I mean you're not really anything more than an exceptionally powerful mage. You've done some amazing things, but up until a few years ago, you were a fisherman's son. Even now, you don't know beast magic. Horgar is probably the best one to deal with this. Maybe telling him is all Sariel wanted you to do."

Jez shook his head. "If that were the case, Sariel could've just gone to Horgar directly."

Lina pursed her lips. "Are you sure?"

"Why wouldn't he?"

"You said he's bound by certain rules."

"Yes."

"Well, Horgar isn't a Shadowguard."

Jez opened his mouth to respond, but closed it after a second. He inclined his head. "That could be it, but do you remember how Shamarion treated Osmund?"

They both nodded. Shamarion had been a Shadowguard they'd encountered during the ordeal in Rumar. He hadn't been rude, exactly. He simply hadn't considered anyone but Jez worth noticing. Sariel might care for humanity as a whole, but Jez doubted he would regard an individual mortal, any mortal, highly enough to entrust with something like this. Jez might only be fourteen, but to a being that had existed since the creation of the universe, fourteen years wasn't really that different from forty, or four hundred for that matter. Sariel wouldn't have even batted an eye at his youth.

"You know," Osmund said, "just because Sariel brought it to you doesn't mean he was right. Have you ever considered it might be a good idea to let others handle this sort of thing?"

Sariel had given this task to him. It didn't seem right to just let someone else do it. Jez's hands curled around empty air, and he realized he was on the verge of summoning Luntayary's crystal sword. His skin was tingling, and he forced himself to calm down. Maybe his friends were right.

"I'm just not sure."

"Are you still going to check the lower levels?" Osmund asked

"I might as well. Besis is going to come by in an hour to take me down there, but I'm starting to think the masters are right. I'm not going to find anything down there, but maybe I can convince Besis to talk to Horgar."

Lina smiled. "You're just not going to let this go, are you?"

"When a pharim lord comes to you and gives you a mission, you don't turn away from it."

Lina sighed and stood. "I'll call my father."

"Why?"

"I was going to go home over the next term, but I'm not going to miss this."

"You don't have to do that," Jez said.

"Yes," Osmund said with a grin. "Please don't. I was really looking forward to some peace and quiet."

She glared at him and flicked a finger at him. A ball of violet light shot toward his face. He cried out and threw up his hands, but the ball passed right through him and vanished behind his head. Jez tried to hold in a chuckle, but he could only manage to keep a straight face for a few seconds before laughter erupted. Osmund scowled at them both, but he couldn't maintain it for long and soon joined the rest of them in laughter. All too soon, though, the reality of the situation settled on them, and their laughter died.

"What will happen if Aniel doesn't return?" Lina asked.

Jez shrugged. "I don't know. It's not like this has ever happened before."

"Beast magic will continue to fail," Osmund said. "That might be the least destructive thing to happen. Aniel doesn't just preside over beast magic. He rules over the beasts themselves. Without his influence, they'll go insane. Even domestic animals like horses will be affected and could even become a danger to us."

Jez stared at him, but of course it made sense that Osmund would have a better idea about these things than the rest of them. Though an adept of destruction, Osmund had spent a great deal of time studying theology, hoping to understand more about where he'd come from. They'd met an afur in Rumar, and Osmund had maintained contact with her, but he still kept up with his studies.

"Are you sure?" Jez asked.

"Not really. Like you said, this has never happened before, but people have theorized about the importance of each of pharim lords.

None, except perhaps Apalel, would be a more devastating loss than Aniel."

Jez shuddered at the thought of the pharim lord of healing going missing, but he pushed the thought out of his mind. Aniel's loss would be bad enough. Much of the world's trade required the use of horses, and cities like Tarcai depended on that trade to survive. Aniel's loss could very well end the Academy itself. Lina pursed her lips.

"If it's that bad, I'm not leaving," Lina said. "You might need my help."

"I think we could do without you," Osmund said.

Lina raised an eyebrow. "You do remember Rumar, don't you?"

"Yes."

"Do you remember the time you would've died without my help?"

Osmund narrowed his eyes at her, and she met his gaze without flinching. Jez let out a breath.

"Lina, go call your parents. Meet me back here in three hours. We'll talk about what to do then."

CHAPTER 12

Jez picked the silk doll off a shelf. It was completely white and looked to be little more than a bundle of silk forced into a vaguely human form. He closed his eyes and tried to sense the creature banished by the binding, but there was nothing. It wasn't really surprising. The phobos wasn't truly inside the doll. The doll was just a talisman bound to the demon, a thing left behind when demons of a certain power were banished. It prevented the creature from coming into the world, but the demon itself was still in the abyss with the rest of its kind. He replaced the talisman among other, similar artifacts. There were hundreds of talismans used for that purpose. He himself had brought many with him when he'd returned from Rumar, but as far as he could tell, everything here served to bind a demon. He saw no sign that any of them held Aniel.

"Not that I would recognize it if it were," he said under his breath.

"What was that?" Besis asked.

The protection master stayed within a few feet of Jez at all times. He'd identified anything Jez had asked about, though there were some artifacts he hadn't allowed Jez to touch. Even with the master's help, however, they hadn't found anything.

"Nothing," Jez said. "You were right. There's nothing down

here." A shiver ran down Jez's spine, and he eyed the demons' prisons. "At least, there's nothing good down here."

Besis nodded and led Jez back up. It took a while since Besis had to pause to disable the wards protecting these levels. The stairs spiraled down around the inner wall of the tower. Each floor was warded with workings that became increasingly deadly the lower you went. In the upper levels, they would provide no more than an unpleasant shock, but the ones three levels down were lethal. The masters took no chances in protecting the things kept here.

Lina was waiting when they came up into the chamber that took up the entire first floor of the tower. As soon as she saw them, she rushed to Jez's side. Besis raised an eyebrow.

"Jez, it's worse than we thought. Beast magic is failing everywhere."

"What do you mean?" Besis asked. "What have you heard?" Lina took a step back at his tone. Besis took a deep breath and inclined his head. "I'm sorry. Please, tell me what happened."

"I called my parents. My father told me about attacks in Quintiar by mages who turned into animals. As soon as I closed the link between him, the speaking stone received another communication." She glanced up at Besis and blushed. "There was no one else there, so I answered it. There were other attacks in half a dozen cities in Nakior too."

Jez grabbed Besis's arm. "Master, you have to talk to Master Horgar. Get him to tell me what he knows."

Besis shook his head. "Jezreel, you know I can't do that. This is in his dominion. I have no authority over him."

"But you have influence. Look at it this way. If people everywhere are suffering from beast mind, who better would there be to help them than Horgar? Anybody can go looking for the cause, but not everyone can do what he can."

"Beast mind can't be cured," Besis said.

"But he can do something, more than anyone else could do. Let me go look for Aniel."

"He won't like it."

Jez threw his arms up in frustration. "I know he thinks I'm just a child—"

"That's not it at all," Besis said softly.

"It's not?"

Besis sighed. "For all intents and purposes, he's just lost three students, one to the testing and two to beast mind. It's almost unheard of for a master to lose even one student in a term. To lose three so quickly is a terrible loss, and the guilt is crushing him. He won't lightly send another student into danger."

Jez met the master's gaze. "Master Besis, there's no one else who can do this."

Besis smirked. "Well, aren't you sure of yourself?"

"Sariel is."

Besis bit back whatever reply he was about to make and looked Jez in the eye. Lina stepped up next to him, as if her presence would help convince the master. Jez tried to pour all his confidence into his gaze, though he wasn't sure if he succeeded. Finally, Besis nodded.

"Very well. I'll do what I can. I only hope you're right."

CHAPTER 13

There was an unusual quiet over the Academy over the next two days. There were fewer people out than normal, even for the time between terms. The town itself became still almost the instant the sun set, and students from the Academy were viewed with suspicion, and few chose to venture into Tarcai. If anyone else suffered from beast mind, Jez didn't hear of it.

Finally, one evening a week later, a heavy knock sounded at Jez's door. He opened it to find Master Horgar. For a second, he just stared. Then, the master cleared his throat. Jez let him in, and they sat at his table.

"I would've come to you if you'd called, Master," Jez said.

"It's of little consequence. Besis regards you highly. He's been speaking on your behalf practically nonstop since the trial."

"I really think I can help."

Horgar spoke softly. "I don't want your death on my head, Jezreel."

"It won't be."

"You seem so sure of yourself."

Jez smiled. "That's not what I mean, Master. I learned a long time ago how important choices are. I make my own. If those choices lead me down a dark road, my death won't be on your head. It'll be on mine."

"You're not making it any easier for me to tell you."

"A high lord of the pharim is missing. This isn't an easy time."

Horgar snorted. "Wisdom beyond your years." He walked to Jez's window and he stared out onto the city. A hawk was circling, and Horgar watched it. Jez shifted his weight, unsure of what to do. Finally, Horgar turned to face him.

"There is a valley in the mountains, fifty miles to the south, where I perform some of my examinations. It is a wild place, ideal for the practice of beast magic. It is almost completely inaccessible. It's where Barash's magic failed, and where I first struggled to transform." Horgar narrowed his eyes. "That is privileged information."

Jez inclined his head. "I understand, Master."

Horgar nodded and pulled out a rolled piece a parchment. He spread it out on Jez's table, revealing a map of the Kelag Mountains. He pointed to an unmarked spot far from any city. "I've been there the past couple of days, but I've found nothing. Maybe you can succeed where I failed."

"If it's inaccessible, how do I get to it?"

"I normally fly," Horgar said. "I'm not sure that's the best solution though. If you transformed, you might not be able to change back."

"I don't know how to transform, so that doesn't really matter." Jez pointed to the large river that flowed through the Kelag mountains. The river's source was near the spot Horgar had pointed to. "It's watered by run off from the mountains?"

Horgar looked at him blankly. "I have no idea. That's not the sort of things I normally pay attention to."

Jez nodded. His study of terra and aqua magic had included learning how the two elements behaved naturally, and that gave him a fair idea of how the land affected the flow of rivers. "It almost has to be. The snow probably melts to create a tributary that feeds the Kuna."

"The Kuna is unnavigable in the mountains. Even if it wasn't, the valley is well above the level of the river. You'd have no way to get up there."

Jez smiled. "Let me worry about that. I'll let Osmund and Lina know. We'll leave by the end of the day."

Horgar started when he heard the names. He looked like he was going to argue, but instead sighed and nodded.

"You may want to stay a day or two. Besis will probably want your help."

"Why?"

The beasts master took a deep breath. "I'm going to make a request of him. I want everybody who's studied beast magic to have their power bound."

CHAPTER 14

Binding a mage's power was difficult work. It involved crafting a ward between a mage and that power. That part was easy enough. Many mages, even those who didn't study protection extensively, learned how to do that to one extent or another. The hard part came with linking that ward to the mage's power so it fed off of it and gave it a measure of permanence. As each mage's power was unique, so the binding of each mage differed from all others. It could take an hour or more to get it right, but once the binding was in place, the mage wouldn't be able to touch their power. That power had become so much a part of Jez's life that even the thought of being cut off from it made him shudder.

Everyone who had the slightest ability in warding was conscripted into helping. There were a surprising number of people who could transform, and it wasn't just those who wore the green robes. Cross dominion studies were common, and nearly a third of the Academy's seven hundred students had to be bound. Most looked at Jez as if he was an executioner, though a couple, mainly those who studied something other than beasts, thanked him. He could see fear in their eyes. They didn't want to lose themselves.

A few people talked of binding Osmund, but Rael convinced

Horgar that Osmund's transformation into Ziary was different and that the scion wasn't subject to the same rules. To Jez's surprise, Osmund didn't seem entirely relieved at being exempt. The entire ordeal took three days. Besis bound Horgar last. When they were done, Jez couldn't help but feel like they had crippled the Academy.

Jez fell into a chair at the Quarter Horse. He stared blankly forward. Osmund and Lina sat across from him, but he barely noticed them. The innkeeper brought him a bowl of hot lamb soup. Jez blinked at him and wondered how the man had known what he wanted, but then he remembered that he'd ordered the same thing the past two nights. The days had started to blur together. He thanked Lufka and started shoveling food into his mouth. He barely noticed the taste as he chewed and swallowed. He was halfway through before he spoke.

"I never want to do anything like that again."

"It had to be done," Lina said.

Jez looked up and managed a weak smile. "I never realized how empty those words sounded."

"What do we do now?" Osmund asked.

"I'm going to rest tomorrow. The day after that, we'll go to Horgar's valley."

"Have you thought of how we're going to get there?"

"That won't really be a problem," Jez said. "We just have to get to the Kuna."

"The Kuna that is impassable?"

Osmund jumped as his own soup began to swirl. It spun faster and faster, but not a drop spilled over the side of the bowl. Manipulating it was more difficult than if it had been the pure element, but aqua magic had always been one of Jez's strongest areas, and making the soup stir itself didn't require that much power. He grinned.

"The Kuna that is made of water."

Osmund grinned and rose to slap his friend on the back before finishing his meal. They didn't stay late because Jez was feeling utterly drained. He returned to his room in a half daze. The sun had just started to set when he fell asleep.

CHAPTER 15

Exhausted from his days of binding powers, Jez hardly got out of bed the next day and left his companions to do most of the preparations. Osmund gathered supplies and Lina spent the day pouring through maps with Master Horgar to get a better idea of where exactly the valley was. Apparently, it was rather difficult as Horgar only knew the route from the air, but eventually, they got a good idea of its location.

The next day, Jez still wasn't feeling completely recovered, but he felt well enough to travel and they bought mules in Tarcai. The stableman was hesitant to sell to children, but he eventually gave in. There were many nobles at the Academy, and while most liked horses, strange purchases weren't really that unusual. The Kelag Mountains couldn't easily be travelled through, so they descended to the city of Hiranta and departed from there, walking through the foothills on the edge of the Korandish Plains.

After three days, Lina recognized a mountain with twin peaks that Horgar had mentioned. They took another day in reaching the landmark before turning and heading into the mountains. Though Jez had spent most of the previous year at the Academy, he hadn't really gone into the mountains aside from Mount Carcer itself, and he had very little idea of what traveling through them entailed. This area was mapped in only the loosest sense. They knew which mountains were where but had very little idea of where they could find passes. Jez tried to sense the way through with terra magic, but the mountains were just too big, and his mind couldn't encompass them. Their sheer vastness overwhelmed him, and he'd fallen to the ground before he let go of his power. Osmund rushed to his side, but Jez waved him off.

"I'm okay, but I won't be trying that again."

Osmund looked up and took a deep breath. "I'll go up. Maybe I can see a way through."

"You're nervous," Jez said. "What's going on?"

Osmund looked away. "It's probably just my imagination. The past couple of weeks, I've felt Ziary stirring. Ever since Barash..." Osmund shivered, and his voice became soft. "I think he might be waking up."

Lina took a step back, and her fingers went to the scar on her cheek. Before he could control Ziary, Osmund had nearly killed her. When Marrowit had put Ziary to sleep, Osmund had gained the ability to control him, but if Ziary was waking up, transforming could be extremely dangerous. The scion would seek to destroy anything it perceived as evil, and even the slightest transgression could earn his wrath. Lina, realizing what she was doing, brought her hand down and forced herself to step closer to Osmund. Osmund nodded at her, but didn't say anything. He sighed.

"Well, it's not like we weren't planning on taking risks. The two of you should hide, just in case."

"We're not doing anything wrong," Lina said.

"Do you really want to take the risk?" Osmund asked.

Again, Lina touched her scar. She nodded, and she and Jez hid behind a nearby bush. Osmund closed his eyes, and wings of pure light emerged from his back. He grew a foot taller, and his red robes seemed to shimmer. Though Jez couldn't see his face, he knew the scion's face was pale, and his eyes had changed into twin points of flame. Ziary launched himself into the air and quickly vanished into the sky.

"Do you think this will work?" Lina's voice was barely above a whisper, as if afraid Ziary would hear her and come looking.

"Yes," Jez said.

"You sound so certain."

"I'm not completely sure, but I don't think Ziary has access to Osmund's memories. If he remembered to take off, it means Osmund is still in control."

Lina let out a breath, and Jez could practically see the tension flow out of her. Absently, she brushed at a twig that had gotten tangled in her hair.

"Was it really that bad?"

For a second, he thought she wouldn't answer, but then she nodded. A tear ran down her cheek.

"It wasn't just the wound. It wasn't even mostly the wound. When he cut me..." She closed her eyes and took a couple of deep breaths. Her lower lip quivered as she spoke. "I saw myself. I was petty and cruel and not deserving of mercy. I didn't deserve to live."

"Don't think that way," Jez said. "Ziary comes from a group of beings whose expressed purpose is to destroy evil. He can only see the bad."

She nodded. "I know that. It's just that sometimes, I don't believe it. I really was petty and cruel, and I was so vain. Sometimes, I wonder if I still am."

Jez shook his head. "You're not. You haven't been for a long time."

"Are you sure?"

"You're here, aren't you? No one forced you to come. You knew it would be dangerous, but you came anyway."

"That's different. If we can't find Aniel, it could be bad for the whole world. It doesn't take a good person to want to do everything she can to help with that."

"When was the last time you used an illusion to cover your scar? You don't even try to hide it with the powders I've seen other girls use."

"What would be the point? I would still have it. There's not really a reason to hide it."

"That's what I'm talking about. That's not something a vain person would say." He smiled. "You know, after we first met, Besis told me you were a spoiled little girl."

Her face went red. "He said that? He's a master. He's not supposed to say things like that about students."

Jez laughed. "Well, you were at the time. You've changed a lot in the past year."

She grinned at him and seemed to calm down a little. "You haven't. You're still an uncivilized peasant boy in over his head."

Jez laughed even harder. "I don't think that will ever change."

A shadow passed over them, and Lina paled. She looked up just as Ziary flew over them. He came down a few feet away from them, and Jez realized Lina had gotten behind him. Ziary's flaming eyes focused on Lina before moving to Jez. The form of the scion melted away leaving Osmund in his place. He pointed south.

"Maybe ten miles in that direction, there's a pass that goes deeper into the mountains. It winds a little, but it eventually hits the river."

"Were you able to control him?"

Osmund's eyes flashed to Lina before nodding. "It's harder than it has been, but I could manage it. I don't know how much longer I'll be able to keep it up, though. I shouldn't do that again unless I really have to."

Lina stepped in front of Jez. She was shaking, but it was only a little. Osmund either didn't notice or pretended not to.

"I'm glad," she said. "I'm sure you'll be able to keep him under control. I've studied a little mind magic. Let me know if there's anything I can do."

Osmund inclined his head, and Jez could tell the words meant a lot to him. The actions Ziary had taken weighed heavily on his conscious. There was nothing Lina could do for him that one of the masters hadn't already tried, but she had practically told him she forgave him. The two of them clasped hands and they headed south toward the pass that would lead them to the river and the valley beyond.

CHAPTER 16

It was another two days of hard travel to get to the river. By the end of it, every muscle Jez had ached. Even riding the mules hadn't provided much help. The animals had become more and more unruly as the days went on. There was plenty of shrubbery for them to feed on, so in the end, Jez let them go to fend for themselves.

The Kuna itself was wide at this point in the mountains. It flowed quickly downhill, its waters churned by the rocks until they were white. The river was fed by dozens of small lakes as well as runoff from the snowcapped peaks. The pass Osmund led them through had wound further south, and according to the map, they were now twenty miles from their destination.

"Well?" Osmund asked.

Jez knelt by the river and dipped his fingers in. The cold water was a shock, but it wore off after a second. He closed his eyes and concentrated, trying to feel something in the water. He jerked his hand back when a turtle, no bigger than his palm, snapped onto his finger. He cried out and shook his hand. The turtle stayed latched on for several seconds before being flung back into the water. He turned and glared at Osmund and Lina who hadn't been able to stay standing because they'd been laughing so hard.

"It's not funny," he said.

"Yes it is," Osmund said between chuckles.

Lina finished her laughter first and wiped at her eyes as she got to her feet. "Are those normally like that or do you think it's because of Aniel?"

Jez shrugged and looked at Osmund, and the larger boy rolled his eyes. "I don't know. The fish in the Kelag Mountains were never a subject I studied. It could just be how they are."

"Turtles aren't fish," Jez said.

Osmund shrugged. "Like I said. I never studied them."

"I think there's something upriver."

"You think?"

Jez narrowed his eyes. "Have you ever tried to detect a disruption in beast magic miles away through a river?"

Osmund smirked. "No, is it hard?"

A spray of water shot out of the river, arcing over Jez and hitting Osmund right in the face. He sputtered and glared at Jez, but Jez only grinned.

"Maybe it was a fish. Come on. Let's go."

Osmund frowned and wiped his face on his shirt. Then, they set off again. Jez had expected travelling along the shore would be easier, but that idea was quickly dispelled. The area around the river was often rough, and more than once, they had to go around large formations of rock. A couple of times, they had to wade into the river itself in order to avoid impassable terrain. The current was so strong Jez was forced to direct the river around them, but moving that much water took a great deal of effort, and he couldn't maintain it for long. Once, when they were traversing a stretch of river fifty yards long, he lost his grip on the water, and the current slammed

into them, driving them back a hundred feet before they could get to shore. They took half a day to rest after that so Jez could recover his strength. In the end, they were able to make it, though only barely. They considered pressing on after that to make the most out of the daylight, but in the end, they decided to make camp and face the next leg of their trip after a full night's sleep.

Jez's dreams were filled with images of birds in flight and wolves running through the woods. He saw the fish in the sea and the worms burrowing beneath the earth. More than anything else, his mind was filled with images of the hunt, the thrill of catching a scent, of running across the ground or tearing through the air, or rushing through the sea, but there was the other side too. Something was after him. Panther or wolf, he didn't know. It didn't matter. He ran. His heart was racing. It wouldn't be enough.

The wolf leapt onto the stag, its teeth closing around the throat. The falcon dove and caught the sparrow from the midst of the flock. The pike surged forward, snapping up the smaller fish. He felt himself dying. He felt himself killing. Fear and exhilaration twined within him, the combined feelings of predator and prey. For the first time, he felt like he knew what it was to be alive.

Jez woke up screaming, not sure if he was excited or terrified. Osmund cried out and jumped back, and Jez realized the larger boy had been shaking him. Lina stared at him with wide eyes, obviously terrified. Jez blinked in the brightness of the sun and realized it was already nearing noon.

"What happened?"

"You started screaming just before dawn," Osmund said. "At least part of it was screams. Other times, you sounded more like an animal."

Jez nodded, and looked to the north. Something within him

stirred. It was like he had caught the scent of prey.

"Aniel is nearby," he said.

"Are you sure?"

Jez's mind flashed back to the wolf and the stag, and he shook his head to clear his mind of the image. He pointed deeper into the mountains. "It's only about a mile in that direction. We should be coming upon a tributary soon."

Osmund frowned. "Jez, you can't know that, not unless the barrier Sariel put on your mind—"

Jez shook his head. "My memories are still locked away. This is something else."

"What?"

"I have no idea. Come on. It's this way."

They packed up their camp quietly and continued on. Though Jez had gotten more sleep than either of his companions, his arms felt heavy, and he kept stumbling over his own feet. After half a mile, they came to a small river five feet wide that was feeding the Kuna. Jez pointed to it, and they followed it until they reached a waterfall that fell into a pool. The rock face was practically sheer, and thick vegetation hung over the edge.

"It's up there."

Osmund and Lina looked up. Osmund let out a low whistle, and Lina stared at Jez for a second.

"How are we supposed to get up there?" she asked.

Jez stared at the waterfall for a second before letting out a breath and shaking his head. "I thought I'd be able to do this, but there's just no way." He looked at Osmund. "Can Ziary carry us up there?"

"No, there's too big of a chance I would lose control."

Jez frowned. "That's what I was afraid of. I'll need a contingent."

Lina paled and her jaw dropped. She took a step back from him.

"Jez, I've been trying to forget the chopping block for six months."

Jez shook his head. He'd had nightmares about that too. In a battle with a human form demon named Sharim, they'd had the image of their heads on chopping block burned into their minds as a way to inflict terror on them. In the end, Jez had realized that the image embedded in their thoughts had been exactly the same, and forming the same image in your mind was the first step in forming a contingent to combine your power. The more complex the image the more completely the powers are joined, and that image had been so detailed he'd felt the wood of the chopping block as his head had been held down. He and Lina had been able to use that image to form a contingent and defeat a demon general.

"I don't think illusion or mental magic will be much help." Jez glanced at Osmund. "Wind might though."

Osmund nodded. "Lina, can you do what Sharim did to us and give us an image?"

"Not the exact same one. Your minds would interpret whatever I did differently. I don't know how Sharim was able to do it."

"I don't need something complex," Jez said. "How about a circle on a grid pattern?"

She nodded. "That might work. The simpler the image the less your mind will interpret it. Close your eyes."

Jez did and the image appeared before him. He focused on it. He could feel Osmund drawing on his power, and Jez moved his own magic until it entwined with his friend's.

"Step into the river," he said without opening his eyes. He held out his hand. "One of you, please guide me. We need to be as close to the waterfall as possible, and I don't want to lose my concentration. Stay together. I don't think I'll be able to do this more than once."

A smaller hand than his closed around his wrist, and he followed Lina to the lake. It was cold, but he ignored it as he sank his power into the water. He could feel the waterfall churning it, and he sent his awareness into the falling water. Much smaller than the entire river, it was easy for him to grip it and redirect its flow.

The water was falling with tremendous energy, and as it reached the surface of the pool, he turned it, directing it upward. Someone gasped, though Jez couldn't tell if it was Osmund or Lina. The water only went half the distance up the cliff before coming under gravity's sway again and splashing back down. Using his power to perceive where they were going, Jez led Lina toward the inverted fall. She resisted for a second before following, and he could sense Osmund a few feet behind. The water was to his chest when she tugged. They were still about ten feet away from the falls.

"Jez, I'm about to go under."

"All right. Hold on."

He twisted the water, and the inverted waterfall twisted like a snake and came up directly under them. Instantly, they were soaked. The water came up so strong that it was painful, and Osmund cried out as the jet of water carried them up. Jez drew on Osmund's power. Wind buffeted them and kept them from falling. Jez forced more of his own power into the water. The jet became stronger and lifted them higher.

"Jez!" Osmund's voice bellowed over the sound of the water. "We're over the waterfall!"

Jez nodded, though he doubted they could see him through the spray. He bent the water, and they shot forward. This time, both of his companions screamed. Jez called the wind, and they slowed, but not by much. Suddenly the power surged and snapped away from him. He opened his eyes just as he crashed into the muddy ground.

He tumbled several feet before coming to a stop. He rolled onto his back and groaned. His bones screamed as he forced himself into a sitting position.

He looked around. Osmund had crashed into a tree, but rather than being hurt, most of the tree had been reduced to splinters. The charred wood around the larger boy said it had been Ziary, not Osmund who had hit it. It was probably the only reason he had survived. Osmund blinked and sat up with considerably less effort than Jez had managed.

Nearby, a bush rustled, and Lina crawled out. Her shirt sleeve had ripped, and she had twigs and leaves in her hair. A bruise had started to form just beneath her left eye, and she winced as she stood up. She walked to him.

"Jez, are you all right?"

He blinked. "I think so."

"You're bleeding."

He reached up and touched his forehead. His fingers came away bloody. He felt sick. "Maybe that wasn't such a good idea."

Osmund managed a weak laugh. "It's about average for your plans."

Jez glared at him, but before he could say anything, a small bird with a long needle-like beak flew in front of him. It hovered, its wings moving so fast he couldn't see them. He blinked and it flew a little ways away to stick its beak in a bright red flower. A line of trees thick with foliage stood several yards off, and Jez stared into them. The sense of familiarity, of prey, had grown even stronger.

"We're here."

Lina offered Jez a hand up and he turned to the valley that, in all likelihood, served as the prison for a high lord of the pharim.

CHAPTER 17

Jez had spent most of his life on the coast of Korand. Then, he'd travelled through the plains and came to the mountains where he'd spent most of the past year. He had never seen a real forest, but he'd always imagined them as nothing more than a group of trees that one could easily walk through. He'd never expected anything like this.

The shrubbery was as tall as Osmund, and vines stretched from tree to tree. Several sprouted the red flowers the bird had eaten from. Even the foliage on the shore of the river was so thick it would be impassable. It was like a great green wall looming before them.

Their supplies had been scattered over several hundred yards, and it took the better part of an hour for them to gather everything up. Among the supplies were three long curved knives that Osmund called machetes. At first, Jez hadn't really understood why they needed them, but after seeing the thick underbrush, it was obvious they'd never be able to walk through the jungle without cutting their way through.

"What do we do now?" Osmund asked.

Jez bit his lower lip and stared into the trees. "I'm not really sure."

Osmund rolled his eyes and grinned at Lina. "You see what I

mean about his plans?"

Jez glared at him before closing his eyes. The prey scent hadn't so much vanished as it had spread out. It was coming from everywhere. He opened his eyes.

"I'm almost positive Aniel is here somewhere."

Osmund made an exaggerated motion of looking around. "Where?"

Jez rolled his eyes and started walking toward the tree line. "If I knew that, I wouldn't have said 'somewhere.'"

"So your plan is to find Aniel somewhere in the jungle?"

Jez stopped in front of a large bush. He turned around and narrowed his eyes. "You can stay here if you want."

Osmund let out a long breath and walked to the underbrush and slashed away a couple of bushes. He turned and raised an eyebrow. "Are you two coming?"

After two hours, they were completely exhausted, and they hadn't even gone a mile. Added to the pain from landing, it left them feeling truly miserable. The air was thick, and sometimes Jez felt more like he was swimming than walking. They were all sweating profusely, and they went through water at an alarming rate. Most of their water skins had been lost, but they stayed near the river, and Jez used his abilities to separate the water from any impurities. According to Lina, it still tasted funny, but Jez was fairly sure she was just looking for a reason to complain. Osmund seemed to be having the easiest time. He wasn't moving much faster than the rest of them, but he didn't need to rest as often either.

"Having legs that long must really help," Lina said after the third time Osmund scouted ahead while they rested.

Osmund shrugged. "Before I left home, I spent a lot of time hiding in the jungle there. This isn't really all that different." He sighed. "I don't think we're going to find Aniel just by walking around though."

Jez cut a vine away from his path before turning to Osmund. "Why not?"

"We've been looking for hours, and Horgar knew this place a lot better than we do. He never found him." Osmund motioned to the trees around them. "Besides, in jungle this thick, we could pass within five feet of an army and not notice it. We're not going to find an imprisoned pharim, particularly not if whoever imprisoned him wants him hidden."

"Do you have a better idea?"

"Did you ever study summoning?"

"A little. I had to summon imps to help new students learn about binding."

"Do you think you could summon a Beastwalker?"

Jez blinked at him. "Are you serious?"

"Can you think of a better idea?"

"I know how to summon minor demons, not pharim."

"It's not like a pharim would hurt you. Shamarion obeyed your commands."

"Shamarion is a Shadowguard. Sariel told them about me. Besides, don't you think Horgar would've already tried a summoning?"

"Horgar isn't a pharim."

"Neither am I." Osmund raised an eyebrow, but Jez shook his head. "I'm not."

"Yes you are," Osmund said. "You are in every way that matters." Lina snorted, but Osmund glared at her before turning back to Jez. "You defeated two demon lords in single combat. If that doesn't make you a pharim, I don't know what does."

Jez shook his head. "Maries was a demon general, not a demon lord."

Osmund rolled his eyes. "Yes, that makes a big difference."

Jez let out a breath. "Even if it didn't, I had help with Maries."

Lina grinned. "Oh, if you only defeated a demon general because you had help, that obviously invalidates Osmund's argument." Her face grew serious. "Jez, you have to admit he has a point."

Jez looked from one to the other before throwing up his hands in surrender. "Fine, I'll give it a try. Just give me some time to work it out. It's not the same as summoning a demon."

It wasn't difficult to figure out how to alter the imp summoning ritual. At Osmund's insistence, Jez had long ago worked out how to bind his scion. The runes needed to do that were many of the same ones needed to affect pharim. It was just a matter of replacing half a dozen runes.

He used terra magic to clear an area of ground roughly ten feet across, but he didn't dare use any mystical means to draw the circle. The magics could too easily interfere with each other. Instead, he used a stick, though he had to start over several times. A circle didn't need to be absolutely perfect to work for a summoning, but the closer the better. Once the circle was done, he set about drawing runes in the dirt. The whole process took two hours, and by the time he was done, the sky had begun to darken. He turned to Lina and Osmund who had set up camp nearby.

"I don't suppose either of you know the name of a Beastwalker?" They both shook their heads, and Jez sighed. A name would've made it easier, but he could probably manage without one. "I can call one, but I don't think I can hold it."

"Do you need to?" Lina asked. "It's a pharim. Aren't they supposed to be good?"

"They're supposed to be watching over beasts. If I summon one who is doing that, I become the thing getting in the way of their duty. That's not something they react too kindly toward."

"Oh," Lina said as she backed up from the circle.

"Should I change?" Osmund asked.

Jez shook his head. "You could lose control. Ziary wouldn't attack a pharim, but he might see me as being evil for trying to summon one. Still, be ready in case we need to defend ourselves." Osmund nodded. "Don't hurt him."

Osmund stared at him for a second before bursting into laughter. It took him a second to regain his composure. "You're worried about me hurting him?"

Jez gave him a half smile. "Good point."

Jez stood at the edge of the circle and raised his arms. He uttered the words of the ritual and the runes began glowing yellow. Jez reached out with his mind, trying to find a target for his summons. He'd never been very good at this, and it was like trying to see through muddy water. He closed his eyes and spoke louder. The air around him vibrated with the power he was sending into the circle, drowning out everything else. He focused, casting out his thoughts in a net meant to ensnare a Beastwalker.

"Jez."

He barely heard the voice over the hum of power, but he didn't open his eyes.

"Beastwalker."

He endowed the word with power and sent it into the circle. The water in his mind cleared a little, but not enough for him to see through it.

"Jez."

The voice was louder this time, but he ignored it. The ritual consumed his mind, and he didn't want to lose his grip on it. He called again but there was no response.

"Enough!"

The voice cut through the buzz, and it was like a boulder splashing into the water. He opened his eyes and gasped. The thing before him had the torso and head of a man, but beneath its waist, it had the lean body of a lion. Its powerful paws clawed at the ground. Its face was surrounded by a yellow mane, and it held a bow with an arrow nocked pointed right at Jez's face.

CHAPTER 18

Osmund and Lina had already been taken prisoner by other animal men. One that looked like a wolf that stood on two legs guarded Osmund while a woman with lizard scales and long curved teeth stood over Lina. Jez could feel the wards blocking them from their power. He knew from experience that such a ward wouldn't prevent Osmund from transforming, but with him in danger of losing control of Ziary, unleashing the scion might be worse than being caught.

Jez felt a ward forming to block him from his power, but he was too quick and crafted a working to draw water from the air. The ward ran into the active working and shattered against it. Jez shrouded his hand in the water and shaped it into claws. He hardened the liquid to the point of being stronger than steel before holding his hand toward the lion man.

"Put down your weapons and let go of my friends," he said.

The creature let out a sound, but Jez wasn't sure if it was a laugh or a roar. Jez sniffed at the air, looking for any sign of the sulfuric smell that would indicate demons, but there was nothing. The lion man curled its lips back to display long sharp teeth. He never lowered his bow.

"Little human boy, at this moment, you are surrounded by the warriors of my pack, many of whom have arrows trained on you. Your command of water is impressive, and you might even be able to take out one or two of us, but no more than that. Don't be foolish. Put away your working and allow yourself to be warded."

Jez let the claws return to liquid, but he kept the water swirling around his hand so as to not allow them the opportunity to ward him. "What do you want from us?"

"I will not speak to someone armed as you are."

Jez's hand went to his waist, but stopped. He was wearing a sword, but it was secure in its sheath, and the curved knife he'd been using to cut through the foliage was with the rest of their supplies. He cocked his head at the lion man.

"Your power, boy. Put away your power and allow yourself to be warded."

"Why would I do that?"

The lion man smirked, showing its teeth again. He circled Jez until he was standing in the circle. He smudged several parts with his foot.

"Because your friends are captive, and you are surrounded. This is a battle you can't possibly win, and any course but surrender will only lead to death."

Jez glanced at Osmund, and the other boy nodded. Jez reached for Luntayary's power, intending to summon one of the crystal swords of the Shadowguard.

"Jez?"

A creature with a body that was vaguely man shaped but with a bull's head stepped out of the brush. Its legs ended in hooves and he had arms thicker than any Jez had ever seen. Long pointed horns protruded from its head. Jez's eyes went wide when he saw that the tip of the left horn was broken, the same one that had cracked when the giant bull had attacked the central spire of the Academy.

"Toden?"

The bull man nodded. "That's what they called me. I remember you. You helped me."

"I helped?"

"I didn't want to hurt anyone, but I was just so mad. I don't even know why I was mad."

"You know this child, Mirous?"

Toden nodded. "He stopped me from killing, Galine."

The cat man looked from Toden to Jez. He lowered the bow, but didn't remove the arrow. Jez threw a glance at Osmund, but the other boy only shrugged.

"Put away the water," Galine said. "Keep your power."

Jez eyed him, but shook his head. "If I'm not holding a working, you can just cut me off."

Galine nodded and waved his hand at the two guards standing over Osmund and Lina. The shields barring them from their power vanished. Instantly, Osmund's arm was wreathed in flame, and Lina vanished from sight.

"There is no need for that," Galine said. "Come, let us talk, and you can tell me why you were trying to summon one of Lord Aniel's children."

Jez and his companions exchanged glances. The beast men were already heading into the woods. Only Toden hadn't moved, and Jez tried not to stare.

"Are you really Toden?"

"I was."

"You were?"

"I'm called Mirous now."

"Why?" Jez asked

Toden pawed at the ground, but he didn't seem to notice what he was doing. "I don't remember much from before, just being angry."

"You weren't an angry person," Lina said. "You were nice. I liked you."

He smiled. "I don't remember being a person." He looked to where Galine had gone. "We should go. Galine can explain everything."

CHAPTER 19

Toden moved quickly through the jungle. In spite of his massive form, the bull man didn't leave so much as a snapped twig to mark his passage. Jez and his companions started falling behind, but Toden stopped to wait for them. The other beast men were nowhere to be seen, and Toden gave them a disapproving stare when they cut underbrush out of their way, but he made no move to stop them.

Day had given way to night before they finally arrived in a large clearing. By then, the pace they were going at had made every muscle in Jez's body ache, but he forgot about that as soon as he beheld the home of the beast men.

A few huts dotted the clearing. Some were human sized, while others had doors twelve feet tall and roofs higher than most manors Jez had seen. A pair of ape men were putting a new roof on one house. Strangely enough, animal dens existed alongside the houses. At one end of the clearing, there was an opening to a cave. Other animal people moved around the makeshift camp, though the line between animal and man varied from person to person. He saw a pair of people who were completely human except for the claws where their fingers should be, and one woman had feathers instead of hair.

Others were almost wholly beasts. There was one who looked like a dog but with a face and eyes that looked all too human. It was an effort not to stare.

Galine was waiting at the other edge of the clearing. Other cat people, the beast portion coming from lions or tigers or panthers, had gathered around him, and his yellow eyes followed Jez as he walked across the clearing. Jez couldn't help but feeling like a mouse being watched by a cat. A panther woman next to Galine bared her teeth, and Jez wondered if she didn't see him the same way. More than one beast man growled as they walked by.

Finally, Jez stood before Galine. The lion man looked down at Jez, and Jez took an involuntary step back. He had to stop himself from summoning his crystal sword, in spite of the fact that all his senses told him these weren't demons. Though his sword was a deadly weapon in its own right, it wouldn't protect him against a hail of arrows.

"Who are you?" he asked.

Galine nodded at Toden. "I would think your friend would make it obvious."

Jez glanced at Toden before nodding. "You're people who suffered beast mind."

Behind him, someone growled, and it was all Jez could do not to turn and look. He had the feeling that showing fear to these people would be a very bad idea.

"Watch your words." Galine's words were closer to a growl than a voice. "We do not suffer."

Jez stammered and took a step back. Immediately, he chided himself for the reaction and forced himself to stand up straight and look Galine in the eyes.

"I'm sorry," he said. "I didn't know."

"Do you know how one is taken by the beast mind?"

Jez nodded. "You stay transformed for a long time. Days or months. The instincts take over, and you stop being human."

A rumble escaped Galine's throat, and Jez realized he was laughing. "A simplistic explanation. We choose it. Every one of us. We found human existence too trying or painful, or unfulfilling. For one reason or another, we were running, looking for something that we didn't know." Galine showed his teeth. "We found it."

Jez looked around at the beast men. Inhuman eyes stared back at him. He returned his gaze to Galine. "All of you?"

Galine nodded. "As you said, one must be in beast form for days or months for this change to happen. Do you think one can stay in another form so long by accident?"

Jez gave Toden a pointed look. "Even him."

"He doesn't know what's happened to him yet. The change into something other than human is trying on the mind. It will be months before he's fully restored, that is, if it happens at all." Galine gave Jez a level look. "What do you know?"

"I know that a few hours before I saw him as a bull, he was human in full control of himself."

"That's impossible," he said.

Jez sighed. "I wish it was. The beasts master doesn't know how it happened. Toden was on the second floor of the Academy tower. Do you think a huge bull just crept up the stairs when no one was looking? He was in his room and he changed without wanting to."

Galine snorted. "Could you accidently write a letter or accidently build a house? It's not something that happens by accident."

"It's why I'm here," Jez said. "I came to find out what's wrong with beast magic."

Galine laughed. It was difficult to tell with his half human voice, but it sounded a little forced. "If there was something wrong with beast magic, we would know."

Behind him, some of the cat people were exchanging uneasy glances. Galine, seeming to sense this, turned and hissed at them. They took a step back and inclined their heads, and Galine returned his attention to Jez.

"Why were you trying to summon one of Aniel's children?"

Jez was about to answer when Lina put a hand on his shoulder. He looked at her, but Lina's gaze was focused on Galine.

"You already know why, don't you?"

Galine shifted his weight, but rather than coming off as nervousness, Jez got the impression he was preparing to attack. Lina either didn't notice or didn't care. She took a step forward seeming completely confident, though Jez could sense the power she held inside. She was one of the most skilled illusionists the Academy had seen in a couple of centuries. In the blink of an eye, she could vanish.

"You could've stopped him at any time. You didn't because you hoped he would succeed. They're missing too, and you know it. Just like Aniel."

Galine snarled, but Osmund stepped up next to Lina. His eyes glowed orange and curls of smoke rose from them. Though he wasn't as tall as Galine, he was every bit as imposing.

"I wouldn't," Galine said. "We're no threat to you, but we can be."

The hairs on the back of Jez's neck stood on end. He turned to see some of the other beast men moving toward them. Some had bows drawn. One, a black furred wolf-like creature that stood on two legs, was only about ten feet away, having moved without making a sound. A trio of other wolf people were right behind him.

"Please, stop!" Toden cried out as he ran in front of the wolf. The wolf snarled and pushed him aside with casual ease, and Toden fell to the ground.

Galine tensed, but relaxed after a second and let out a long breath. "There's no need for this."

"But they know," the wolf said as he took another step toward Jez.

"They knew before they ever met us. I suspect that means others know as well. This isn't something we can hide."

"Why would you want to?" Jez asked.

"Say nothing, Galine. We don't know if we can trust him," the wolf man said in a voice that was closer to a growl than anything else.

"Don't be foolish, Welb. We can't very well expect them to keep a secret if they don't know why."

"We don't have to let them go at all."

Galine took a step toward Welb, pushing Jez out of the way in the process. Jez flew two feet to one side before coming down in a puddle of mud. For a second, he could only gape at the lion, astonished at his casual strength. The two beast men stared at each other. Their growls were echoed by everyone in the clearing, though none of the others moved. The sound made the ground rumble, and Jez felt the power in their combined voices.

The feather haired woman threw her head back and let out a screech. The beast men let out howls and roars, and the jungle echoed their calls. Welb was broader in the shoulders with thicker arms, but Galine didn't seem to care. Welb's muzzle snapped forward. Galine moved only slightly, and Welb's jaws missed him by inches. Galine's massive paw shot forward in an orange blur. It slammed into Welb's throat. The wolf man grunted as he was lifted off his feet. Galine let out a roar and slammed Welb into the ground. The beast men went silent, and Galine showed his teeth.

"We will tell them." Galine's voice was like thunder, but when he looked up at Jez, his eyes looked kind. "Please, have a seat. There is much we should discuss."

CHAPTER 20

We are the guardians of this place," Galine said, "entrusted by Lord Aniel himself. It is a place of power. You know of such places?" Jez nodded, and Galine continued. "One with the skill can tap into that power and do terrible things. We have been charged to ensure that does not happen. This is not the only such place in the world, and many are watched over by Lord Aniel's children, the ones you know as Beastwalkers."

Jez understood. "And you don't want us to tell anyone because if the word gets out that the Beastwalkers are missing..."

Galine nodded. "Men would descend on the places the Beastwalkers were set to watch, and few who would seek such power can be entrusted with its use."

"Do you know what happened to them?"

"Only that they vanished after the loss of our speaking stone."

Jez blinked at him. "You have a speaking stone?"

"We had one. It allows us to speak to the Beastwalkers directly."

Jez and his companions exchanged glances. "I didn't know a speaking stone could do that."

"This one could. It vanished a few weeks ago. We tried other means to contact them, but nothing worked."

"There something you're not telling us," Lina broke in. "Where did this all happen?"

For a second, Galine looked shocked, but Jez smiled. "She's very good at that."

"Your huts are new." She waved at the roof the ape men were building. "So are those dens, and you're building others. You haven't been in this clearing for very long."

From the ground, Welb snorted. Galine looked at him but didn't offer him help getting up. The wolf man rolled onto his stomach and slunk away. Before Welb disappeared into the jungle, he turned and glared at Galine.

"You have always been too human, Galine. If you wish to return to them, you need only reverse your transformation."

Galine snarled but Welb vanished into the trees. A handful of others, many with wolf features, followed, but most remained. Galine stared after them for several seconds. Finally, Jez cleared his throat, and Galine returned his attention to them.

"It's nothing you need to concern yourself with. I won the challenge."

"What did he mean when he said you only need to reverse the transformation?" Jez asked.

Galine sighed. "We all were taken by the beast mind and were all forcibly turned back to human. It doesn't work, not with our minds no longer human. Eventually, we were brought here and given these forms where our minds could find balance."

"Who brought you?"

"The beasts master at the Academy, mostly."

"Master Horgar?"

Galine nodded. "And Master Gwyna before him. L'tarro before her, going on for as long as anyone can remember."

Jez looked over his shoulder at Toden who was helping the ape men with the roof. "Then, reversing the transformation is turning back into human?"

"Yes."

"You mean you could just go back?"

Galine shook his head. "Only in body. Being taken by the beast mind changed us irreversibly. Our thoughts are a mingling of animal and man. My mind is like that of a lion. It will always be, and a human brain simply isn't capable of dealing with it. Neither can the body of a beast deal with the mind of a man."

"If a beast can't deal with the mind of a man, how do people transform?"

"It's difficult to explain to one who doesn't even study the dominion. Essentially, transformation magic holds the mind in flux and makes it something the beast can deal with. Ours no longer can."

"So you're stuck like this?"

"We have made our peace with it." He closed his eyes for a second. "At least I thought we had."

"What do you mean?"

Galine inclined his head to Lina. "Your friend was correct. We have not been in this clearing for very long. Our tribe used to be much bigger than this, but most of us went mad after the speaking stone disappeared."

"Maybe that's a place to start," Jez said. "If someone stole your speaking stone, they might have contacted Aniel and led him into a trap."

Galine barked out a laugh. "You think someone trapped him?"

"It's possible."

"Do you think it's such an easy thing to trap a pharim high lord?"

"It's just a place to start. I might be able to see something you missed."

"Or smell it," Osmund said.

A dog woman yipped and Jez turned, but she had her face averted. The way her body moved told him she was trying not to laugh. Jez looked back to Galine who was looking from Jez to Osmund.

"Do you imagine you can smell what we cannot?"

"It's a different kind of smelling," Jez said.

Galine pulled back his lips and showed his teeth. "It's extremely dangerous. The mad ones are still out there. The power of a beast mixed with the mind of man can be a formidable danger."

"We can take care of ourselves."

"Very well. I'll lead you to the site of the old village in the morning."

CHAPTER 21

It was difficult to sleep. Though the soft patch of grass Jez lay down on was comfortable, the air was so thick he felt like he was being smothered, and he sweated constantly. His shirt clung to him, and he struggled out of it, but it didn't do much to cool him. It was closer to dawn than dusk when he finally fell asleep.

He screamed when he woke up to a creature with round eyes too big to be human and a curved nose. The creature hopped back and Jez sat up. He blinked several times and saw that the thing that had woken him was another of the beast men, though it was closer to being an owl than a man. He pursed his lips. It might actually be a beast woman. He couldn't really tell which.

He took several deep breaths. The dreams had been back, and he'd hunted and been hunted half a dozen times. He could practically still taste the blood. He looked around. The beast men were going about their business. Galine was speaking to a pair of birds, and Toden was nowhere to be seen. No one was staring at Jez, so he didn't seem to have screamed in his sleep. His stomach growled. Osmund was seated on a stump munching on a handful of berries. When he saw Jez away, he waved at a pile of fruit that sat nearby on the ground. Some had been sliced, and Jez didn't recognize what most of them were. Still the sight made his mouth water.

Jez sat up and picked up a slice of fruit that had red skin and orange flesh. He bit into it, and flavor exploded in his mouth. It was sweet, a little like an orange and a little like a pineapple. Juices dripped down his face, and he gobbled it up and took two other pieces as well. The old baron Dusan had had a fondness for exotic fruit, and so Jez had been exposed to more variety than most, but even he had never seen so many. There fruit of every shape and size, each with its own unique flavor. Even the ones he was familiar with had odd tastes to them, infinitely better than the fruit he'd eaten before.

"This is all so amazing."

Osmund smiled as he popped a red berry into his mouth. His teeth had been stained by the fruit. "Just like home. Fruit always tastes better when it's fresh."

"If the two of you are done," Galine said as he walked up to them. "I can take you to the old village." He smirked. "Of course, if you think sitting here filling your bellies is more important than finding the missing pharim high lord, I can understand that as well. The fruit is, I'm told, quite good."

"You haven't had it?" Jez asked. Galine showed his teeth, pointed and ill-suited for plants. "Oh, right."

"I can always go on without you," Lina said. "It would give you a chance to finish eating."

She was perched on a nearby rock. A pair of new water skins hung from her waist, and she'd torn the sleeves off her shirt. Her pack bulged with supplies.

"You're up early," Jez said.

"I couldn't sleep very well." She swatted at her arm and left a small red streak. "The bugs wouldn't leave me alone."

"You should've said something," Galine said. He waved a hand, and grimaced. He tried again, staring at Lina for a second before finally nodding. "There, they shouldn't bother you anymore."

She raised an eyebrow. "Thank you."

"It's failing for you too, isn't it?" Jez asked. "Beast magic, I mean."

Galine pulled back his lips, but nodded. "Probably less than it is for you, but we'll lose the ability completely before long."

"What'll happen to you?"

"We don't know. Most think the rest of us will go mad." He let out a growl. "We're desperate, or I wouldn't have accepted your help. So please, finish your meal and let's go."

Jez nodded. The beast men had prepared new packs for each of them as well as fresh water skins, and they started off after Galine. Almost instantly, he left them behind, and it took them five minutes to find him again. He scowled, but didn't say anything and continued into trees, though he moved slower than before. This time, it was a full five minutes before they lost him.

After the third time Galine was forced to stop to wait for them, Jez was frustrated. He couldn't understand how the huge creature could move through the woods so quickly. Galine shrugged when Jez asked him about it. He couldn't explain it saying only that it was instinct and that all beast men could do it.

"I'm not used to your kind anymore. I'll go slower."

"How far are we?" Lina asked.

"I could make it in an hour, but at the speed you move at? A day, perhaps two."

Jez nodded, and once again, they started after Galine. It took a day and a half, they reached a clearing and Galine stopped. The faint murmuring of a brook sounded form just beyond the trees, many of which bore colorful fruit. Though it was still early in the day, this seemed like a perfect place to make camp.

"Are we going to rest?" Jez asked.

His legs were aching, and he was breathing heavily. Galine shook his head.

"We're here."

"Here?"

Jez looked around. There was nothing in the clearing, but as he gave the area a closer examination, he saw the signs. Several trees on the other end of the clearing had been torn out of the ground. Though underbrush had started growing into the clearing, Jez could see that the moss covered mounds were the remnants of buildings. Something had upturned the ground. Vines covered something vaguely human shaped at one end of the clearing, and Jez didn't want to see what was under them.

"Be careful," Galine said. "We're not alone."

Before Jez had a chance to ask what he was talking about, something brushed passed his leg. He yelped and jumped back as a huge snake rose out of the grass. It was longer than he was tall, and near the head, its body flattened out, forming a hood. It hissed at him, tasting the air with its forked tongue. Its long curved teeth dripped with venom. Jez raised his hands and backed up slowly but stopped when he bumped into something. He turned to see another of the snakes, this one at least twice as long as the first. Other snake creatures rose from the grass, though some were closer to being human than serpent.

"Friends of yours, Galine?"

"They were once," Galine said, and claws emerged from his fingers. "Then, they went mad. Prepare yourself to fight, but be careful. If you let them bite you, you'll be dead before you hit the ground."

CHAPTER 22

Jez drew his machete and slashed at the snake creature nearest him, but the blade bounced of his foe's scales. The thing lunged at him. Its head moved in a blur, and he fell back. The creature's bite got so close he could feel the wind of its passage. Jez cried out at the sound of its teeth snapping together. He drew his sword and struck as he fell. Sharper than the machete, it left a shallow gash on the snake's torso. It hissed and drew back, and Jez manage to get to his feet before it recovered.

Another Jez appeared a few feet away, though this one was armed with a crystal sword. Beside him was another Osmund and Lina. Other images appeared until there were four of each. Only Galine remained unduplicated.

"I can't keep this up for very long," One of the Linas said. Jez had no idea if it was the real one.

"Get away from here, Lina," Osmund cried out. "We'll hold them off."

A solid figure touched Jez's shoulder and he glanced over his shoulder to see Osmund standing back to back with him.

"Just like in Rumar," Osmund said. "Don't you think you should use your other sword?"

Jez considered for a second before shaking his head. "They're not demons."

One of the creatures darted forward, but a quick slash of Osmund's sword sent it reeling.

"Half snake, half man," Osmund said. "If they're not demons, they're close."

"Not the same thing." Jez's words tumbled over each other as he turned away another attack. "You could change, though."

"Maybe if I wanted to kill you and Lina both. Ziary is barely dozing now."

"We don't have a small army with us this time."

"I know."

"So basically, it's nothing like Rumar at all."

"We're probably going to die. That's kind of like Rumar."

"That's not really comforting," Jez said as he slashed upward with this sword. The blade tore open the stomach of a snake man.

"She hasn't left yet," Osmund said.

Jez looked around. Galine, taking full advantage of the distraction provided by the illusions, had already taken down three of the snakes, but the illusions were still moving too precisely to be a working that had been left in place. Lina had to be nearby directing them.

Most of the fake Jezes and Osmunds also fought back to back. Surprisingly, when their blades hit the snakes, the creatures hissed in pain. Jez hadn't realized she could do that. A good illusionist could create a tactile illusion, making sensations that felt just as real as if they were actually being experienced. Sharim had done that to him once, and he winced at the memory. The blades did no real harm though, and even an illusionist of Lina's caliber could only maintain so many illusions at once.

"We need to go on the offensive," Osmund said.

"Hold them off me," Jez said. "I have an idea, but I need a few seconds."

Osmund slashed at one before spinning around so he was facing the same direction as Jez. He threw one hand forward and a blast of wind shot out driving the snake men back. Then, he turned just in time to catch a snake man who nearly sank its teeth into his arm.

The momentary reprieve was all Jez needed. The thick humidity in the air had made Jez feel like he was being suffocated ever since he entered into the jungle, but he used that now as he drew the moisture out of the air. Water swirled around him in a whirlwind. One of the snakes got close, but a miniature geyser shot out from the ground at Jez's feet and struck it in the face so hard it fell to the ground, unconscious.

Jez spread his arms and the whirlwind grew wider, knocking out snake men as it slammed into them. Illusions flickered as the water touched them, and the real Lina cried out and reappeared. She glared at him, completely soaked, but Jez stayed focused on his working. The water spread out thirty feet before splashing to the ground. Jez fell to his knees, breathing heavily. The world was spinning before him. The air was so dry, it burned his throat, but it didn't take long for humidity to return. Galine went to him and shook himself in the same way a dog might. Finally, Jez was able to stand.

"That was unpleasant," Galine said. "Cleverly done, but unpleasant."

"Did I get them all?"

"You almost got me too."

"Sorry," Jez said as he managed to sit up. "I don't know you as well as the others. You were harder to recognize."

Galine looked over the clearing of fallen snake men. "Given the circumstances, I won't hold it against you."

"But you recognized me," Lina said as she wiped her forehead to stop water from dripping into her eyes.

Jez managed a smile. "Well yes, but it would've taken more power to exclude you. I wasn't sure I'd have enough to make the working big enough. You wouldn't have wanted me to fail, would you?"

She glared but didn't say anything. Galine cleared his throat, and Jez looked at him.

"Come, let's see to them before they wake up."

Osmund had a rope in his pack, and they cut it into pieces and used it to tie the snake people's arms, as well as the legs of those who had them. As Jez tied the last one, he took a deep breath and drew back so fast he almost tripped over his legs.

"What is it?" Galine asked.

"These things smell like sulfur. I think they've been possessed."

CHAPTER 23

They lined up the snake men, and Jez walked up to the largest one. Now that he knew to look for it, he caught the faint smell of sulfur hanging about the creature. He put his hand on the snake man's forehead and closed his eyes. A chill ran through him, and his awareness brushed against something wrong, something that didn't belong in this world.

He concentrated, but he couldn't tell what type of demon it was. He splayed his fingers and touched the snake man's forehead. As he dragged his hand down to the creature's heart, he pushed power through his fingertips. The snake man stiffened, and its scales emitted a soft blue light. It opened its eyes, but rather than the slitted eyes of a snake, they looked like sapphires shimmering under the light of the noonday sun. The snake man arched its back and let out a cry that was neither human nor snake. Black smoke billowed from its mouth and began to take shape. Before it could congeal, however, Jez waved a hand and the smoke scattered as the demon was banished back to the abyss.

The snake man took in a sharp breath but closed his eyes again. Rather than moving on to the next one, Jez examined him more closely. He ran his hand over the head and torso of the creature, searching with every sense he had.

"What is it?" Osmund asked.

"There's something else wrong with him," Jez said. "Give me a minute." It was another few seconds before he found it. He opened his eyes and pulled his hand back. "There's a darkness inside of him that doesn't feel natural."

"What do you mean 'darkness'?" Galine asked.

"I'm not sure." He met Galine's eyes. "This balance you mentioned. It's a working of beast magic, isn't it?"

Galine shook his head. "Not exactly. There's a working in our minds that helps make the first step, but everything after that comes from us alone."

Jez nodded. "What would happen if that working were corrupted?"

"What would happen if you removed the roots from a tree? Everything built atop the working would eventually collapse."

"Something similar to beast mind?"

"Maybe."

Jez looked at the unconscious snake man. "I think that's what happened to them."

"No, impossible. Even if the working failed altogether, it would take time for something like this to happen. Maybe if it was just one, I could believe it, but practically everyone who went mad did so at the same time."

"They had help," Jez said. "It's not easy for a demon to inhabit mortals and control them, but a person transformed by beast magic with the foundation of their minds crumbling? It might not be enough for them to be controlled right away..."

He let the words hang and Galine inclined his head. "They wouldn't really need to be controlled. If the demon drove back the conscious mind, they would revert to something..." he motioned to the snake men. "Like that. Can you free the rest of them?"

"I think so," Jez said as he moved on to the next one.

The second didn't take as long as the first, and the third was even faster, but it still wasn't quick enough. He was only three quarters of the way through before they started to awaken. Osmund threw himself at the last one while Galine held down two with his massive paws. They struggled to rise as Jez pulled the demons out and dispersed them.

The last one screamed as Jez drew out its demon. By then, the rest of the snake men were up and looking at each other, trying to figure out what was happening. Galine spoke to them quietly while Osmund and Lina stood over Jez as he leaned against a tree to rest. After a few seconds, one of the snake men, close enough to human to have arms and legs, approached them. Osmund's hand began to glow slightly, flame flickering around his fingers. Jez knew he was ready to attack, but the snake man ignored him and focused on Jez. He had a scar across the left side of his face. It had cut through his eye and left it completely white.

"I am Ravous." His voice was gravelly, and he drew out the 's' sound. He bowed deeply to Jez. "Thank you."

"Please don't do that. I'm Jez. Can you tell me what happened?"

Ravous shook his head. "We don't know. All any of us can remember is going to sleep. After that, there are flashes of anger." He looked at the fallen snake men, the ones that Galine had taken down in the fight. None of them were moving. He looked at the half lion. Galine's shoulders slumped, and he kept his head down. He didn't look up when Ravous spoke.

"Thank you as well, Galine. I would not have wanted to live that way. Neither would they."

Galine shook his head and spoke softly. "You can't speak for the dead."

"It was like when the madness came upon us, before we had found balance. No one would choose to live that way."

"If it was the madness, it could've been cured."

"It wasn't the madness," Jez said. "It might've been like the madness, but it was something different."

Galine snarled at him. "What do you know about the madness?"

"I know it's not caused by demons." Jez cocked his head. "Okay, I don't actually know that. Is it?"

"It's the beast mind and the human mind fighting one another," Galine said.

"Well, you saw what came out of them," Jez said.

Galine sighed and looked away. He walked to the edge of the clearing and stared into the woods. Jez could barely make out the low rumble escaping from his throat. Jez's gaze stayed locked on the beast man for several seconds.

"What's wrong?" Lina asked.

"He killed," Ravous said.

"But he's a lion," Lina said. "Lions kill."

"Lions hunt," Ravous said. "They protect their territory. They defend themselves. They don't do this."

"But he was defending himself," Lina said.

"Why did he bring you here?"

"I wanted to see the old village," Jez said. "I thought I might be able to find something you all missed."

Ravous hissed. "It is a human reason."

"Well, yes. I'm human."

"He is not, though he has often been accused of it."

"The wolf," Jez said.

Ravous nodded. "Welb has been Galine's greatest opponent since he took over the tribe. It will not help him to have it known that he killed for a human reason."

"What if we don't tell anyone?"

The snake man smiled, and Jez found himself taking several steps back. "Were I the leader, that might work, but not him. He has never been one to lead from the shadows. He will inform the tribe himself."

Jez was nodding before Ravous finished speaking. Such a thing felt right to him, but Lina pursed her lips. "But that's foolish."

"Lions are proud creatures, and I suspect that as a man, he was no different."

"Will he be okay?" Jez asked.

"Perhaps. His leadership will be weakened, but he may survive it."

"Do you think Welb will try to take over?"

"No. He complains a great deal, but he's had the chance to take leadership before and has always found a way around it." He gave Jez that evil looking grin. "Like my kind, wolves prefer to work from the shadows. There are others who might challenge him though."

"Others who might not like working with us?"

"Quite possibly. I myself would not associate with you if you hadn't saved us."

Jez nodded. "Can you show me where the speaking stone was?"

The snake looked to Galine, but the lion man didn't turn from the woods, so Ravous nodded. He led them to a group of trees. Underbrush had grown thick between them but the snakes cleared it away. The raised receptacle had almost been covered by leaves and branches, and Jez had to look close to see that it wasn't a natural formation.

"It sat on that."

Lina blinked at him. "You just had it out in the open?"

"Who would steal it?" Ravous asked.

Jez took a deep breath, but he caught no whiff of sulfur. He extended his protection sense but didn't find anything. He turned to his friends.

"Look for anything. Use all your senses."

They each nodded and closed their eyes. Jez had limited proficiency with dominions other than protection, but he used what little he had. When he got to his sense of knowledge he felt a prickle against his awareness. He walked over to one of the trees and brushed aside a branch to find the image of a tooth and claw carved into the bark. He moved on to the tree next to it and found another rune. Others had been chiseled into rocks. Still others had been burned into the grass. Too much time had passed for him to be able to tell what exactly those had been, but he could guess.

"It's a summoning circle."

"What?" Osmund asked.

He indicated the runes he'd found. "Check the trees. All of them."

As more runes were uncovered, Jez grew worried. By the time they'd revealed enough for him to get a good idea of what the circle had been intended to summon, he'd broken out in a cold sweat, and his mouth had gone dry.

"If they did try to use the speaking stone to lure a Beastwalker here, it didn't work."

"What makes you say that?" Osmund asked.

He pointed to the first rune he'd found. "That's a circle used to summon a Beastwalker by force."

The snakes hissed, and one went into the jungle to get Galine. The lion returned a few minutes later. He examined the runes and growled. "Who could've done this?"

Jez and Osmund exchanged glances. Osmund's eyes widened and he opened his mouth to speak, but Jez shook his head.

"No, it can't be him."

"He is a skilled summoner," Osmund said, "and we already know he can use places of power." He glanced at a rune on a nearby tree before looking back to Jez. "He can trap pharim too."

Lina had paled and brought her hand to her neck.

"What?" Galine said. "Do you know who did this?"

Before Jez had been born, the dark mage Dusan had battled the Shadowguard Luntayary. Dusan had lost, but had lashed out at the pharim, cursing him and binding him to human flesh. A stillborn child had been given life, and Luntayary had been born as a human, but the reason Dusan had been able to improvise that working was because he had done it before. He'd caused a demon to be born into the form of a human, unbound by the laws that normally restricted its kind. Unlike Jez, that being had full memory of who and what he was.

"Sharim," Jez said. "I think it's Sharim."

CHAPTER 24

Who is Sharim?" Galine asked.

"He's an extremely dangerous mage," Jez shook his head and started pacing back and forth between the trees. "No, he's more than that. He's a demon made flesh. He almost dethroned King Haziel and toppled Ashtar. It took everything we had to stop him." Jez shuddered. "We almost didn't make it."

"It's not necessarily him," Lina said.

Jez stopped and let out a breath. "You're right. It could be anyone who knows how to tap places of power and is a summoner skilled enough to call and bind a pharim." He shook his head. "Even if it's not Sharim, it's someone nearly as dangerous."

"What do we do?" Osmund asked.

Jez considered for a second. "Where is the center of this place of power?"

"The nexus?" Galine showed his teeth. "Why do you want to know?"

"That's where whoever did this will go."

Galine shook his head. "We have that place watched constantly. It's our first and greatest duty."

"This person was able to take your speaking stone from inside your own village. Sharim could craft illusions good enough to fool even a Veilspeaker. Are you so sure he won't be able to get through your defenses?"

"It is forbidden."

"That wouldn't stop Sharim."

"I'm sorry." Galine looked away. "After what you did, I'd tell you if I could, but I have my commands from Aniel himself, and I will hold to them. I may not reveal the location of the nexus."

"Do you have to stop us if we find it on our own?" Osmund asked.

Galine looked at him for a second and smiled. He shook his head. "No."

"I'll fly up and see if I can find anything."

"Are you sure?" Lina asked. She started to take a step back but stopped herself.

"It's our best option."

"But if Ziary is waking up..."

"I think I can control him. I won't take long. I'll just fly up and come back down."

"Still, maybe you shouldn't." Jez glanced at Lina and couldn't help but look at her scar. "You haven't lost control in over a year, but what you did then still bothers you."

"I know," Osmund said, "but it's a high lord of the pharim. Have that binding ready."

Lina's hand didn't go to her scar as it might once have, but her fingers twitched. She nodded. "Should we hide?"

"Probably," Osmund said.

"Hide from what?" Galine asked. "What's going on?"

"Osmund is a limaph," Jez said. "He has a particularly strong scion, but he can't always control it. When he can't, it's generally best to stay out of the way."

"I see," Galine said.

He waved at Ravous's kin, and the snakes seemed to melt into the trees. Galine retreated into the jungle and vanished as completely as if he'd worked an illusion. Jez glanced at Lina.

"I thought he'd try to stop us, but he didn't. He wanted to tell us where the center was. Do you think that means Ziary will find something?"

"Or maybe he didn't try to stop him because he knows Ziary won't," Lina said.

"I'm right here," Osmund said. "You don't have to talk about me like I'm not here."

Jez grinned. "Technically, we were talking about Ziary, not you." He motioned to Lina and got behind a nearby bush. She followed. "We're ready whenever you are. Please, try not to make me use that binding."

Osmund nodded and turned away. He shimmered, and Ziary appeared. Abruptly, the jungle went quiet save for the wind rustling through the trees. Ziary scanned the area like a predator looking for prey, and Jez got the feeling the rest of the jungle understood this and had gone quiet to avoid attracting attention. The scion's eyes passed over their hiding place before spreading his wings and lifting off. He crashed through the canopy, leaving a few spots of burned leaves in the trees.

For a long time, Jez and Lina sat in the bush without saying a word. Lina kept searching the sky for Ziary. Her hands were shaking, and she was holding her breath. Jez was ready to unleash the binding at a moment's notice.

"It'll be all right," he said.

She point to a gap between the leaves. "There. I see him."

Jez looked up just in time to see Ziary streak between the leaves of the canopy. A few seconds later, the trees rustled and Ziary landed a few feet away, his burning eyes locked onto them. Slowly, he drew his sword. He took a step toward them, and stepped into a puddle, the water turning to steam at his touch.

"Osmund?"

Ziary blinked. When he opened his eyes again, they were Osmund's steel grey. It only lasted for a second before they blazed to light again.

"This place belongs to Aniel and his like. You do not belong here."

Jez's mouth went dry. His fingers danced as he started to weave Ziary's binding, but he hadn't anticipated the scion being so close. Ziary's sword pressed against Jez's neck, and Jez's hands froze. The fires surrounding the blade singed his neck. Jez resisted the urge to cry out.

"None of that," Ziary said. "I should run you through. You trespass on the lands of a high lord of the pharim."

Jez took a deep breath, and moved a fraction of an inch back. Ziary should've killed him. The scion had no comprehension of mercy. There was no reason for him to hesitate. All he understood was that evil had to be destroyed, and he saw even the slightest infraction as evil. "Why haven't you?"

Ziary blinked. "What?"

"Osmund, don't let him do this."

"I am not Osmund," Ziary said, but his sword winked out of existence.

Lina stood quietly and raised her hand as she gathered power. Ziary's gaze shot toward her. A gust of wind blew her off her feet. She flew into a tree and wind held her there. Flame erupted around

Ziary's hand and he pointed it in Lina's direction.

"They are welcome here," Galine's voice came from the trees. A second later, the lion man stepped out of the underbrush. "There is no crime."

"No," Ziary said, his voice sounding desperate. "Authority is given to you to guard this place against intruders, not to welcome them in."

"Osmund," Jez said again. "There is nothing here for you to kill."

The flame reached for Lina, and Jez prepared to bind him, but after a heartbeat, the flame vanished. Ziary's robes dimmed and the fire in his eyes went out. His form shrank as he sank to his knees. When he lifted his head again, tears streamed down a face devoid of any sign of Ziary.

"I'm sorry," he said. "I'm so sorry."

His last word was drowned out as the animals of the jungle renewed their cry. Jez offered him a hand up. Osmund took it, though he refused to meet anyone's eyes.

Galine led them away from the ruined village to a spot by the small stream Jez had heard before. The beast man went off to hunt while the others continued to plan. Jez and Lina spent nearly an hour trying to comfort Osmund before he was willing to say anything that wasn't an apology.

"I almost killed you."

Jez wasn't sure which of them Osmund was talking to, but in the end, it didn't really matter. He knew Osmund wouldn't be comforted by the fact that it hadn't really been him, so Jez needed to try something else.

"Osmund, you can't be blamed for what you almost did." Osmund shook his head, but Jez went on. "Did you see anything?"

Osmund nodded. "I think so. There were lines of...something. I don't know. Power maybe. They were running toward a large lake near the northern edge of the valley. The energy was clumped together there."

Jez looked to Galine, but the lion man just stared at him without saying a word. Jez took that as confirmation and looked back at Osmund.

"Can you lead us there?"

Osmund's expression hardened. "We just need to follow this river. We're only a few hours away."

CHAPTER 25

To Jez's surprise, Galine went with them. Ravous, however, led the snake people and returned to the new city of the beast men, worried that the damaged working on their minds would allow them to be controlled. Jez tried to engage Galine in conversation. The beast man was willing to talk about most things, but anytime Jez's questions strayed too close the nexus of the valley, he stopped talking and refused to say anything for several minutes. As they followed the river upstream, Osmund seemed more and more uneasy. He would jump at every sound and kept looking over his shoulder. Lina was nervous too, though her unease seemed to be due to Osmund, and more than once, Jez caught her rubbing at her scar.

"We're being watched," Galine said.

"By who?" Jez asked.

Galine growled. He lifted his nose and sniffed at the air. Jez did the same, searching for any sign of demons, but he just smelled the earthy scent of trees and grass. Galine, however, tensed his body and looked ready to strike.

"Galine, what is it?"

The trees on the other side of the river began to shudder. Jez drew his sword, but before it was all the way out of its sheath, the trees just behind them started to shake as well. The birds in the trees had gone silent.

"How many are there?" Jez asked.

Galine sniffed. "Six on the other side of the river. Seven behind us." He waved his hand away from the river. "Five a few yards that way. There are more in the branches, but I can't tell how many."

"You mean we're surrounded."

"Completely. Come, we can't let them come at us from all sides. There's a rock face a hundred yards ahead of us. It's the only defensible area we have a chance of reaching."

"Lina, hide us," Jez said. "Don't forget smell."

She nodded and murmured under her breath. The jungle darkened a little as her working hid them from sight. The sounds around them became dull.

"Let's hurry," Lina said. "This isn't very effective."

"Why not?"

"I don't just have to hide us. I have to hide the plants we move aside and our footprints in the ground. There's a lot more happening than the last time I did this."

Jez nodded and they tried to hurry through the trees. They hadn't even covered half the distance when a wolf howled. They couldn't see it, but it couldn't be more than a few yards away. All around them, others echoed the call.

"Keep going," Galine said. "I'll try to lead them away."

Before Jez could respond, the half lion bounded into the jungle. He roared, but it was cut off a second later. Jez rushed forward, leaving the area shrouded by Lina's illusion. He found Galine on the ground.

The thing that stood over him might've been a wolf, if wolves

grew to be six feet tall and had jaws big enough to snap a man in two. Osmund and Lina joined Jez a second later, though Lina had dropped her illusion. Galine struggled to get up, but the massive paws of the wolf held him to the ground. Jez raised his sword and moved to help, but before he had gone a single step, another of the wolves stepped out of the trees and bared its teeth. Two more appeared behind him. Once again, Osmund got to Jez's back and tensed as he prepared to fight. Lina's eyes glowed and Jez almost gagged on the smell of rot that filled the air. The wolves began to whimper and Jez smiled.

"Good job, Lina. You should hide."

She shook her head. "The fewer illusions I have to maintain, the better."

Jez was going to argue, but the wolves stepped forward, and Jez breathed deeply. Beneath the illusion, he caught the faint smell of sulfur.

"I guess that answers that."

He dropped his metal sword, and summoned his crystal one. His flesh started to tingle as he tapped Luntayary's power. As if sensing what the blade meant, the wolves drew back. Even the one standing on Galine retreated a little. The lion man got to his feet, and moved to stand near Jez and Osmund. Blood mingled with the fur in his chest, dripping from a shallow gash just below his shoulder blades, but he seemed otherwise uninjured. He eyed Jez's sword, and gave him a toothy smile.

"Now, that's an interesting tool. Can it stop them?"

"Not all at once."

"Can you do that thing with the water?"

Jez shook his head. "Not if they're half as tough as they look. I could barely handle the snakes."

They were surrounded now. At least twenty pairs of eyes looked from the trees, but they were held at bay by Lina's illusion.

"Lina, how long can you keep this up?"

She grinned. "It's only one sense, and I don't have to vary it at all, so it's not difficult. I can hold it for hours."

"Look."

Galine pointed to the wolf that had knocked him down. It took a single step and sniffed. Then, it gave a growl that made Jez took a step back. It moved forward a little more.

"It bothers them more than it bothers us," Jez said, "but it's not actually stopping them."

The others started closing in and Osmund pulled a six foot blade off of his back. His eyes glowed orange and fire wreathed his blade.

"It's not Ziary's blade, but it's better than nothing."

"Four against twenty," Jez said. "We've faced worse odds."

Other sets of eyes appeared behind the wolves, but the creatures that stepped out of the forest stood on two legs. They were far smaller than their four legged counterparts, but they too had the head of wolves, and their growls shook the leaves. There were at least as many of the two legged wolves as the four legged ones. The lead one was Welb, and he stared at Galine with an almost tangible rage.

Jez glanced over his shoulder at Osmund. "How about four against forty?"

The wolf that had attack Galine let out a howl and leapt at Jez from twenty feet away.

CHAPTER 26

The wolf soared through the air, but Jez's sword darted forward, cutting a slash across its flank. As one, he and Osmund moved aside, and the wolf landed right where they'd been standing. Red blood spurted from its wounds, and Jez froze for a second, shocked. He'd thought these things were demons, but demons didn't bleed.

The wolf threw back its head and howled. A cloud of smoke and flame erupted from its mouth, and the blood running down its side became burning embers. The wolf collapsed to the ground, and the cloud became a pile of ash. The wolf returned to normal size and didn't move. A mortal being did not easily survive a strike from a pharim's blade.

"They're not demons," Jez said. "They're possessed!"

Galine grabbed another wolf out of the air. Using its momentum against it, he threw it over his shoulder into another of the creatures.

"We're too badly outnumbered. Does that make a difference?"

"Not really."

Another wolf leapt at him, but then a two legged one crashed into it, knocking it to the ground and holding it there. In spite of his smaller size, the newcomer had no trouble holding the animal to the ground. The wolf man looked up and grinned at Galine.

"Welb?"

The other wolf men had engaged the larger creatures, and the one under Welb snarled. Welb's muscles tensed and he bared his teeth at Galine. "I'm not going to let you die here."

"Capture them if you can," Galine cried out. "They can still be saved!"

Jez knelt down to draw the demon out of Welb's prisoner. When he looked up, three of the wolves were already on the ground, bleeding and probably dead. Lina was distracting a pair of them by causing bright lights to appear in their eyes. Osmund held them back with wide swings of his burning blade, while the wolf men engaged their larger counterparts. It took four of them to hold one down. Jez banished his sword and rushed to the captive wolf. He ran his hands down its body, drawing the demon out. He nodded at the wolf men, and they released their captive and engaged another.

Jez lost track of time as he ran from one downed wolf to another. Most tried to snap at him, but held down by the wolf men, they couldn't focus their attacks, and Jez avoided them easily.

Out of the twenty, only eight were taken alive. Each demon was harder to draw out and even harder to disperse. He was getting more practiced at it, but he was nearing the limits of his strength. By the time he freed the last one, it was all he could do to remain standing. As smoke came out of the last one, Jez tried to disperse it, but his power slammed against a wall. He tried to seize the demon, but it slipped through is fingers and began to congeal into the form of a large spider.

"Osmund, help."

A ball of fire shot forward, hitting the spider just as its glossy black carapace solidified. Its squeal sent chills down Jez's spine. The fire expanded as it consumed the demon, leaving an oily smell in the air and a blackened mark on the ground.

"Lotheen," Jez said between heavy breaths. "Web weavers."

"Those are the most common possession demons, aren't they?" Osmund asked.

Jez shook his head. "You're thinking of the lothine. They're both spider demons, but the lotheen can make the creatures they possess stronger. I've never heard of so many gathered in one place."

Welb growled and stalked right up to Jez. "You did this!"

Jez almost rolled his eyes, but thought better of it at the last second. With Welb in such a mood, it probably wouldn't be a good idea to antagonize him. Still, after the demons, he just couldn't bring himself to be afraid of Welb. "How could this possibly be my fault?"

"It didn't happen until you got here."

"Yes, it did," Galine said. Welb bared his teeth, but Galine snorted. "You know as well as I do that most of our people went mad long before he got here."

Welb glanced south before narrowing his eyes at Galine. "That's no excuse to take him...there."

"I'm not taking him there. He's taking me."

"It's forbidden!"

"It's forbidden to lead them, not to accompany them."

"Send them away," one of the wolf men said.

Jez blinked when he realized it was a woman, though she looked much younger than the rest. Something in her eyes prickled his memory, and his eyes went wide. He'd never really met her as she'd spent most of her time in the beasts district, but he recognized the girl from the trial.

"Grita?"

She stared at him for a second before shaking her head. "No.

Grita is gone. I am Rouwglar. Grita was a killer. I'm not."

Jez looked around at the wolf men surrounding them before returning his gaze to Grita.

"Are you sure?"

She yelped and glanced at Welb.

"Stop confusing her. She hasn't shaken off the influence of your world."

"She seems closer to being rid of it than you are, Welb," Galine said.

Welb gave him a hateful glare. "When Aniel hears of this—"

"It will mean we know where he is. If he wishes to punish me, he's welcome to."

"I won't let you do this."

Galine's back straightened. His hybrid form towered over the wolf man, but wild fury showed in Welb's eyes. Most of his companions encircled him and Galine, though a few hung back with Grita. Galine looked around and growled.

"This is not how things are done. In a challenge, we fight one on one."

Jez could barely understand Welb through the growls. "You have no supporters here, Galine, and wolves hunt in packs."

Jez tried to call water out of the air, but freeing the wolves had taken all he had, and he slumped against a tree. Lina raised her hand and her eyes glowed violet, but Galine waved her off.

"No, I will not betray our ways," he said without taking his eyes from Welb. "Humans alone choose to go against their nature."

The growl Welb let out made the leaves shudder. Jez could feel its vibrations in the air. Welb bent his knees slightly as he prepared to jump at his opponent. Galine sneered.

"Will you fall to the beast mind again? Will you forsake balance?"

"I don't need to prove myself to you. I know what I am."

"A wolf."

"Yes."

Others howled in agreement. Even Grita was caught up in it, but they all went silent when Galine raised a hand. A few exchanged glances, as if surprised that they had obeyed the gesture.

"Before we are man or beast, we are servants of Aniel, Welb. You would do well to remember that."

"Aniel commanded—"

"He commanded nothing about stopping humans from reaching the nexus. He only said we were not to lead them there. I would not presume to speak for him. Would you?"

The wolves looked at each other. Much of their confidence had drained away. Welb's muzzle dipped so slightly Jez barely saw it, but it was an acknowledgment.

"When Aniel returns, my followers will tell him of this."

"When Aniel returns, I'll tell him myself." He turned back to Osmund. "After you."

Osmund nodded and walked toward one of the wolves. The creature growled, and its fur bristled, but at a bark from Welb, it moved aside. Jez and Lina followed him, and Jez could feel the eyes of the wolves watching him as he passed. He met Grita's eyes for a second, but she turned away, and Jez sighed. He turned his back to her and followed his friend into the jungle.

CHAPTER 27

I was sure they were going to attack," Jez said as he cut away a low hanging branch in his path.

Galine shook his head. "There was no real danger of that. Even if Welb would have, he never could've hidden the fact. One of his followers would've talked."

Jez remembered the look in Welb's eyes and shuddered. "Do you really think he would care about that?"

"A challenge for leadership is done in single combat. So many against one would've been disgraceful, and he never could've held the position. It might even have been the end of him."

Osmund looked over his shoulder at them. "You know, it wouldn't have been just one."

"I'm afraid you don't count."

Osmund's nostrils flared. "Really?"

"Take no offense. You are not of Aniel. My leadership of the tribe may be weak, but without the support of the traditions set down by the Beastwalkers, his would be nonexistent."

"I thought he didn't want leadership."

Galine shrugged. "Maybe he changed his mind."

"We're almost there," Osmund said.

Jez blinked at him. "How do you know?"

Osmund stopped. He pursed his lips and stared into the jungle. He spoke softly. "I can feel it."

"I didn't know you had sensitivity to beast magic."

Osmund took a deep breath. "Neither did I."

"Why wouldn't he?" Galine asked.

"What do you mean?" Jez asked.

"He transforms. How do you think he does that if not with beast magic?"

"But I don't transform into an animal," Osmund said.

"What does that have to do with it?"

"Wouldn't I have to if I were using beast magic?"

Galine let out a bark of laughter. "Beast is a dominion, not a school of magic."

"I know that, but what does that have to do with anything?"

Galine snorted, and he eyed Osmund's blade. The metal had been distorted by the heat of Osmund's working. "What is destruction magic?"

"Fire and air. Physical enhancements to make myself stronger and faster."

"It's more than one thing, but all the things deal with destruction."

"Yes."

"Beast magic deals the beast, not just with animals."

Jez and Osmund exchanged glances before Osmund responded. "What's the difference?"

"Aniel governs the primal forces of life, and few things in all of creation are more primal than true scions. It's beast magic that brings them out."

Jez and Osmund exchanged glances. Lina's jaw dropped a little.

"Can beast magic help me control him?" Osmund asked.

Galine shook his head. "Beast magic has never been about control. Even the animals can't be forced to work against their will. They have to be convinced."

Osmund's shoulders sagged. "Oh."

"We might be able to help you find a balance. That could quell his violent tendencies permanently."

Osmund's gaze snapped to Galine. He stared at him for several seconds. It might've been Jez's imagination, but Jez thought there were tears in his eyes. "Really?"

Galine shrugged. "Ziary may be physically much stronger than the animals we transform into, but his mind is not so different. The animal wants food and water. Ziary wants to destroy evil. They're the same thing, from a certain point of view."

Jez blinked at him. "What point of view is that?"

Galine laughed. "Come stay with us when this is all done. Two months of training with our methods, and I think you'll surprise yourself with what you can achieve."

Osmund nodded, and his smile faded a little. "Maybe I will, when this is all done."

He slashed through a heavy bush and pushed through it. On the other side, they came to a dip in the land. Beneath them was a shallow slope that ended in a lake of water so still that it looked to be made of glass. A peculiar peace fell over Jez. Even the sense of predator and prey he'd been feeling since he arrived in the valley quieted. A gentle breeze blew, though it didn't stir the water. The lake wasn't at all like the waters off the shores of Randak, but Jez couldn't help but be reminded of home.

"What's that in the middle of the lake?" Lina asked.

He blinked. That didn't make sense. This lake was pure. He didn't know how he knew, but he was sure there shouldn't be anything in it. As he looked out over the water, however, he realized she was right. There was something on the water's surface, though it was too far to tell what it was. Jez reached into the water with his power, but pulled back as soon as he touched it. It seemed almost sacrilege to use his magic on the water directly. He turned to Osmund, and the other boy nodded. Osmund raised his hand, and the trees rustled as wind blew through them.

The thing in the water began moving toward them. The water didn't even ripple as it moved, and it took Jez a few minutes to realize that it wasn't on the surface, at least not entirely. It was floating in the lake, though it disturbed the water no more than the wind did. Brown feathers were spread on the water.

"It looks like some kind of bird, but I've never seen one that big." Jez looked to Galine. "Have you?"

"A few, but not of that color. Bring it closer. Nothing dead should be in that lake, though. The waters should have absorbed it."

"Jez cocked his head. It's acid?"

"It's the essence of life."

As the body drew closer, they made out a vaguely human form wearing brilliant green robes that almost seemed to shimmer with their own inner light. Brown fur covered its body, and a curved sword with a white blade hung at its waist. It was face down, though they could just make out a muzzle beneath the surface of the water. Jez could only stare. A rumble escaped Galine's throat. The body washed onto the shore, and they ran to it. Galine reached down and grabbed its shoulder to flip it on its back.

If this being could stand, it would've stood well over six feet. Its face was like that of a bear, but it seemed leaner. Its hands ended in meaty paws with four wicked looking claws at the end. It didn't wear shoes but had the massive paws of a grizzly bear. Jez told himself it couldn't be what he thought, but Galine's voice dispelled his hope.

"That is the body of a Beastwalker."

CHAPTER 28

For a long time, they stared at Galine, unwilling to ask the question that was on all of their minds. The body held Galine's unwavering attention. Jez finally broke the silence.

"How can that be? Pharim can't be killed, at least not in this world."

"I don't know, but I recognize him. That is Talos I've spoken with him often."

"Should we..." Osmund looked away from the body and turned to Galine. "Should we bury him?"

Galine stared at the body for several long moments. Finally, he shook his head. "He always wore the aspect of a bear, and bears do not bury their dead. I would not have him left like that on the shore, though. Push him back into the water. Let the lake have him. Even the birds won't disturb him there."

Jez glanced at the weapon. "What about his sword? That could come in handy."

"Have you ever wielded a pharim's weapon?" Galine asked.

Jez sputtered for a second, not quite willing to reveal his secret to the beast man. Osmund stepped forward. "I've held Ziary's."

"Then perhaps you understand why that isn't possible. The blade of a pharim is linked to their power, and only they can use it. Perhaps if you were a Beastwalker, you could wield his claw blade and not be destroyed. I doubt even another pharim could do the same."

"But he's dead," Osmund said.

"Do you really want to try to use a sword linked to a dead pharim of life?"

"Well..."

Galine shook his head. "I doubt you could touch it without being driven insane. No, push him back into the water, blade and all."

Osmund nodded. Instead of calling the wind, he picked up Talos, and being careful to avoid touching the blade, he placed the pharim gently into the water. The body began to float toward the center of the lake as if carried by a current they couldn't see. After a few minutes, it had become the indistinct figure they'd seen when they'd first arrived.

They all just stared at the body for a long time. At some point, Jez's mind went from disbelief to trying to figure out how such a thing could be done. The power of a pharim wasn't in the mortal realm. If their physical form was destroyed, their consciousness would retreat back to where their power resided, the Keep of the Hosts. Like demons, pharim couldn't be killed.

But Jez had killed a demon.

The year before, when the demon lord Marrowit had been summoned into the mortal world, he'd been fought off by the pyromages of the Academy, and his physical form had been destroyed. He'd retreated into the dream world to recover, and Jez had followed him, battling and defeating the demon in his own center of power. Marrowit, having nowhere else to flee, had been destroyed. Jez sighed.

"What is it?" Osmund asked.

"I was just wondering if the Keep of the Hosts has been invaded."

All three of his companions stared at him with wide eyes. Osmund had gone pale and Lina was shaking her head. Galine finally spoke.

"You think he was killed there and brought here?"

Jez bit his lower lip and thought for a second before shaking his head. "No, it doesn't make sense. If that had happened, we would've been told."

"Told?" Galine asked. "By who?"

"We would've been told," Jez said again. "I think Talos came into this world fully. They can do that if they need to."

"Why would he do that?"

"Maybe to access his full power," Osmund said. "Maybe he was fighting something that needed it."

Jez nodded. Lina looked like she was going to be sick, but Galine shook his head.

"If it were something like that, we would've known."

Jez nodded, and his worry lessened slightly. Galine was right. An erupting volcano could've more easily been hidden than a pharim fighting at his full power.

"What if he didn't come here fully?" Lina asked.

"He has to have," Jez said. "Unless the Keep of the Hosts has fallen, he couldn't have been killed otherwise."

"I know that. I mean what if he was forced? Could he have been summoned fully?"

Jez shook his head. "Not against his will." He paused. "Not unless the summoner had a great deal of power."

"Power like is contained in that lake?"

Jez thought about that for a second. He closed his eyes and reached for the water, but his senses came up against a wall, vaster than a mountain and just as impenetrable. He opened his eyes and looked to his companions. Osmund started to speak, but Jez ignored him and stepped off the shore. His legs sank into the water without making so much as a ripple.

Galine cried out, but his words seemed far away and indistinct. The noises of the jungle faded into the background, and even the sun shining overhead seemed to dim as the lake began to speak to him.

Galine had been right when he'd described this as the essence of life, but that only began to scratch the surface of what the water was. The lake was a source of life, but not in the way the lion man thought. The lake understood the predator and the prey. It knew the excitement of the chase and of the flight, for even the elk felt exhilaration when it escaped the wolf.

"You gave me the dreams," Jez said, unsure if he was speaking with his mind or with his mouth. "You wanted me to come here."

Jez saw himself along with Osmund and Lina, walking through the foothills of the Kelag mountains. Then, Ziary soared up to find a way to the river, and Jez used his power to bring them into the valley.

"I'll take that as a yes," he said.

Joy welled up inside of him, and in his mind, he saw images of the sea, and of all the creatures within. Then, there was a wide river stretching across the land, carrying life wherever it went, and then there were the smaller rivers that fed the larger one, and then there was this lake with Jez standing in it and his friends shouting from the shore.

"What can I do to help?"

A wolf wandered into a jungle. There were too many sights, too many smells. Jez clutched his head. When he opened his eyes, the jungle was gone, and men shot arrows at the wolf. Pain lanced through its shoulder, and it howled before the vision vanished

"I don't understand."

A shark larger than any Jez had ever seen cut through the water. There was nothing such a creature feared. There was a shadow in the water ahead of it, and it rushed in that direction.

Suddenly, Jez was yanked out of the water. He blinked and vision returned to him in a rush. Osmund deposited him on the shore and started shaking him.

"I'm all right." Jez tried to stand, but Osmund kept on shaking. "Why did you do that?"

"You weren't responding, and that," Osmund pointed out to the water, "was about to eat you."

Jez followed where he was pointing, and his jaw dropped. The shark which he had assumed was just a part of his vision was rushing toward the shore. Unlike everything else that had entered the lake, the animal churned the water with its passage.

"But sharks are salt water animals." Osmund blinked at him, and Jez realized how foolish he sounded to bring that up now. "Sorry," Jez said. "The lake flooded my mind with visions. I'm still a little out of it."

The shark reached the shore and jumped. Jez gaped, and Galine growled. The thing was huge, at least a dozen feet long. It went up five feet. Water droplets glittered in the sun, looking like miniature stars. At the peak of the shark's jump, it changed.

Its gray scales gave way to deep brown fur. Its tail split, forming a pair of thick legs that ended in cloven hooves, and the creature landed lightly on the ground. It had the torso of a man, though one that was covered in fur, and its hands gave way to long sharp claws. A pair of curved horns sat atop a head like that of a great cat and three sets of wings, brown like those of an eagle, rose from its back. It stood nine feet tall and at its waist hung a curved sword that

looked like a claw. Its blade was bigger than Jez was tall. The creature looked down at him with slitted eyes like those of a snake.

Instantly, Galine was by Jez's side and looked up at the newcomer. He inclined his head slightly in a gesture of respect, and relief washed over Jez. Lina, having realized who this was, started to bow, but Osmund caught her. She looked at him, and he shook his head. He'd made that mistake once before. One did not bow before a high lord of the pharim.

"My lord Aniel," Galine said. "I am glad to see you again."

CHAPTER 29

Aniel, what happened?" Jez asked. "Where have you been?"

The pharim lord cocked his head at Jez, but didn't answer. His eyes flickered to Osmund, then to Lina, and finally to Galine. Jez glanced at Galine who looked confused.

"My lord?"

Aniel's eyes widened, but he didn't say anything. He ran his finger down the side of Galine's face. His claw left a shallow cut, but the beast man seemed not to notice. Aniel examined the blood on his claw. Jez stepped forward and touched Aniel's other hand.

It was like touching a bolt of lightning.

A crystal sword appeared at Jez's side and his clothes changed to shimmering blue robes. Luntayary's power burned just beneath the surface, and it was all Jez could do to avoid being overwhelmed by it.

"Aniel," he said again, and the snake-like eyes focused on Jez. "Why did you call to me? Do you need help?"

Aniel threw back his head and let out a sound that was halfway between a howl and a roar. The uproar that followed was deafening. It was like all the animals in the jungle cried out in response. Aniel leapt over Jez, transforming into a stag in mead jump. He landed and immediately dashed into the trees. Galine bounded after him leaving

Jez, Osmund, and Lina stunned. They stared at each other for a few seconds before following as quickly as they could, which, given the thickness of the jungle, was little faster than a brisk walk. Aniel left even less of a trace than Galine did, and it didn't take them long to lose the trail. After a few minutes of fumbling through the underbrush, a roar sounded over the noise of the jungle, and all the other animals went silent. Jez forced his way through the trees, and with every step, the smell of sulfur increased. He held out his hand and called his crystal sword.

"Osmund, be ready to change."

"Jez, you know I can't control Ziary."

"I also know he always attacks demons first. Lina be ready to—"

"Help," she said firmly. "I'm not going to hide and let you leave me behind."

Jez smiled. "I was going to say be ready to blur my form like you did in Rumar."

"Oh," she said. "Sorry, I thought..."

"You're one of us, Lina. I'm not going to send you away just because you're not the best in a straight fight. You've already more than proven yourself."

She blushed. "Thank you."

"There will be demons, though. Be ready."

Lina nodded, and Jez could sense the power welling inside of her. Another roar tore through the trees, this one much closer. His crystal sword sliced through the undergrowth as if it was made of paper, and after a few minutes, they came into an area of scorched earth at least a hundred yards wide. A circle of glowing yellow runes shone at one edge, with a small stream flowing through its center. Aniel was walking around its perimeter and gave the occupant a hungry look. Galine paced by his side, his face twisted in barely controlled rage.

Inside the circle stood a boy with raven black hair and pale eyes. As soon as he saw Jez, he lowered his arms.

"Jezreel." His voice had a dry, raspy quality it hadn't possessed before. "I wondered if you would come here." His eyes focused on Aniel. "And I see you've brought me a gift, a high lord of the pharim no less. You have my thanks. You have no idea how hard it is to capture one of those."

Jez didn't bother to reply. He raised his sword and charge at Sharim, the demon made flesh.

CHAPTER 30

Jez had only gone a few steps before Ziary surged passed him, moving in a blur of flame. The scion reached the circle before Jez had covered half the distance. His flaming sword streaked toward Sharim. Sharim didn't even flinch as the sword crash against a wall of green energy. Ziary bellowed again and again, but Sharim's defenses held. Jez stopped before he reached it, and Sharim looked at him and grinned.

"Dusan used that working against us too," Jez said.

"Who do you think taught it to him?"

Jez's fingers began weaving a complex pattern, and he returned Sharim's grin. "I didn't know what I was doing then, but I've learned."

Energy shot from Jez's hands. The barrier in front of Sharim shattered just as Ziary's blade was descending again. The demon cried out and fell back, but the flaming sword sliced into his cheek, cauterizing the wound as it cut. Lina snorted.

"Let's see how he likes it."

Again, Ziary struck, but Sharim raised his hand, and a flaming blade of his own appeared. Gouts of fire shot out of the blades as they impacted with one another. Bat-like wings emerged from

Sharim's back and swept Ziary's legs out from under him, but Ziary's own wings caught him and prevented him from falling. The distraction allowed Sharim to get to his feet, keeping his blade between him and his foe. Ziary rushed forward, his sword moving at a blur. Aniel stepped in beside him while Galine tried to move around the battle to attack him from behind. Jez rushed forward with sword raised.

Sharim took a step back, and a circle of fire appeared around him. Jez was still five feet away, but the heat drove him back. Through the flames, Sharim glared at Ziary. He reached down and ran his fingers over a large leather sack on the ground. His eyes glowed green, and a similar light shone through the hole in the sack and struck the scion.

Ziary stiffened. He turned to Aniel who had gone back to circling Sharim. A quick slash of Ziary's sword left a blackened mark on the pharim lord's chest. Galine cried out, and Aniel drew back in surprise.

Jez froze, but only for a second. He threw his hands forward. A stream of bubbles floated toward Ziary. The first one hit and spread out into a clear filmy substance along the scion's back. Ziary didn't even notice, but then a second one hit, and then a third. With each one, the filmy material expanded. It covered his wings before Ziary realized it was there. He tried to move them, but they were frozen in place. Ziary turned to Jez, his eyes blazing an angry red, but he only had a chance to take one step before the film encompassed him completely.

Galine gaped and Aniel cocked his head. Sharim, taking advantage of the distraction, leapt into the air, his flight having the same erratic pattern as a bat. Aniel's eyes followed him for a second. A growl escaped his throat, and the pharim lord spread his wings. One flap sent out a rush of wind that lifted Jez off the ground and threw him a few feet. A heartbeat later, the pharim lord was in the air, his powerful wings quickly closing the distance between him and his prey. Sharim reached into his sack and pulled out a green crystal as big as Jez's head.

Galine gasped. "It's our speaking stone."

The crystal began to glow. The lake pulsed, and a bolt of emerald energy shot forward from Sharim's hand and struck Aniel. The pharim lord arched his back and let out a piercing cry that, even from so far away, made Jez have to cover his ears.

"No," Jez said once the sound faded. "That's not a speaking stone. That's a focusing crystal."

Sharim disappeared in the distance as Aniel writhed in the air. His wings seemed to melt away. His body thickened, and his arms and legs became hoofed feet. His curved horns straightened as his head became that of a bull. The creature cried out as it fell.

"Jez, let Osmund go!" Lina cried out.

There wasn't time to do anything else, so Jez complied. The film around Ziary shattered, and the scion took to the air. He threw his hands forward and glowed nearly as bright as the sun. A whirlwind appeared around the falling bull, slowing its descent.

The bull cried out and tried to paw at the air, but to no effect. It landed on the grass with little more than a gentle thump, and the animal examined its legs as if unable to believe what had just happened. Then, the bull looked at Ziary and snorted. Ziary arched his back and cried out in pain. His body seemed to shrivel away, and in a few seconds, Osmund stood in his place. The larger boy fell to his knees, but waved off Lina when she tried to help. He stood up without any apparent difficulty. Jez looked into the sky where Sharim had disappeared.

"We have a problem."

CHAPTER 31

Your speaking stone is a focusing crystal?" Jez asked.

Galine shrugged. "If it is, I never knew."

"Where did you get it?"

"It was before my time." He nodded at Aniel. "The stories say he gave it to us when he established our tribe."

"I thought you said beast masters of the Academy established it."

Galine shook his head. "They support us, and most of our members are brought by them, such as your friends, the wolf and the bull, but Aniel brought the first."

Jez turned to the pharim lord. "You gave them a focusing crystal a hundred times larger than any other?"

Aniel let out a sound that might've been a purr. He stepped forward and lifted a hand to Jez's forehead. Jez started and took a step back, but Aniel growled. Jez looked at Galine who nodded.

"I've never known him to hurt anyone who didn't deserve it."

"You know, we aren't really supposed to be here, and he doesn't seem right in the head. He might think I deserve it."

"No, I think he still understands you."

"You think?"

Galine narrowed his eyes. "Jez, this is Aniel, high lord of the

Beastwalkers. You came here for him, and I think he's trying to give you what you want. If you don't do this, you may not find what you're looking for."

Jez eyed Aniel who still stood with his hand extended. He seemed not to be bothered by Jez's hesitation.

"Maybe you should call Sariel," Osmund said.

Jez shook his head. "He wouldn't be able to do anything. He can't interfere with another pharim high lord."

"Not even to help?"

"Not unless Aniel asks for it." He looked the lord of the Beastwalkers up and down. "I don't think he can do that right now."

Jez took a deep breath and nodded at Aniel. The pharim lord took another step forward, and rested his hand on Jez's forehead. The world vanished.

\#

The creature the Hunter sought was more dog than man. It wandered in places the Hunter did not like, among buildings in the cities man had built, but the creature was still of the Hunter. It was one of his children, so the hunter put on the form of a man and went into the city to retrieve the creature.

He attracted many looks. His skin was far darker than any of theirs, and he wore animal skins. He was also taller than most, and he had muscles that one only developed running through the woods or soaring in the sky, so most stayed out of his way.

The creature was a pitiful shadow of what it should've been. It had been living off of trash for weeks and had been reduced to little more than bones. One of its legs had been broken at some point and had never healed correctly. It growled at the Hunter as any dog might if they had been so abused, but this creature's rage had little to do with how it had been treated. It had the mind of a man and the mind of a dog, and the two warred for dominance.

The Hunter extended his hand and sent a thin trickle of power into the beast, calming its twin minds. He took the creature in his arms, and took it to a place between places, emerging in a valley far from the sight of man, a place where a portion of the Hunter's power dwelled. There he started to change the creature back into a man, but not all the way. The creature's mind had been altered, and the only way to give it a measure of peace was to find a balance. He changed it into a dog that walked on two legs.

"Make a place for your kind," the Hunter said, "those who have been taken by the mind of the beast. I will send others to you. Guard my power."

"How do I do this? I know the magic of the beasts, but I am not strong enough to fight those who would claim your power."

The Hunter considered this. Then, he reached into himself, trapping the strength of his own mind. That strength congealed in his hand, and he concentrated it, forcing it into physical form until it had crystallized. He gave the crystal to the one who had been both a man and a dog, and was now a blending of the two.

"Use this to call my children if you require aid, but only with the greatest need should you use its strength to do battle. It is a power not meant for mortal hands."

The Hunter's new servant bowed deeply, but the Hunter grabbed his shoulder. "You need not bow to me nor to any created being, not ever again."

CHAPTER 32

Jez took in a sharp breath. He was on the ground, shaking. He sat up and stared at Aniel. The pharim lord looked confused and glanced at Galine. Lina knelt by Jez's side, her legs covered in the mud from the shore. She was rubbing her forehead. He blinked at her.

"What happened?" he asked.

"You fell over when Aniel touched you, and you wouldn't wake up. I tried to go into your mind to help, but whatever he did wouldn't let me in." She wiped at a thin trickle of blood that had dripped from her nose. She blinked at her bloody fingers. "I guess trying to do that after freeing Osmund from Sharim's control was a little too much."

"How did he do that anyway?" Jez asked. "I thought beast magic couldn't be used to control."

"It can't," Galine said.

"He used mental magic," Osmund said as he offered Jez and Lina a hand up. "I really wanted to kill Aniel. He must have used beast magic to get around my defenses. Your turn Jez. What happened to you?"

Jez looked to Aniel. "He showed me how he founded the tribe. He created the focusing crystal out of his own power to help defend this place."

"Why didn't we know about it, then?" Galine asked.

"I don't know. I'm not sure how long ago that was, but he warned the first beast man to use it only to contact the Beastwalkers, and not to access its power directly except as a last resort. Maybe it was just forgotten. It's not an ordinary focusing crystal though. It can work with power on a level I've never even heard of before. It's made from Aniel's own strength of mind."

"That explains why this Sharim was able to force him to change."

Jez nodded. "We can't let Sharim have something like that. Who knows what he could do with it?"

Osmund eyed Aniel. "What do we do with him?"

"Take him with us," Galine said. "We go hunt our foe and Lord Aniel can help defeat him. Sharim fled from him, after all, so he must fear him."

"Sharim got far enough away to use Aniel's own power against him. There's one other thing to consider." He pointed at Aniel's chest. The burn mark had vanished, but Jez gave a pointed glance toward the center of the lake where the dead pharim floated. "He could be vulnerable. If we take him against Sharim, he could die. What do you think would happen then?"

Galine nodded. "We could leave him with the tribe."

"I don't know," Jez said. "They're a tribe of beast men. If Sharim shows up with a part of Aniel's power, do you really think they'd be able to stop him?"

Galine stood up straight. He didn't take his eyes off of Aniel as he spoke. "They would fight to a man to defend him. They might not succeed, but it's a better defense than any we can provide."

Jez nodded. "It's better than nothing. Let's head back. Maybe we can think of how to find Sharim on the way."

Osmund pointed to the circle. With no one pouring power into it, it had gone dormant, and the runes had gone dim. "Shouldn't we do something about?"

"Good point." Jez eyed the circle. "It looks like a summoning circle, not a binding one." He pointed to a group of squiggly lines. "Lotheen. He must have been summoning them to possess the tribe."

"That doesn't make sense," Galine said. "The first of the tribe went mad weeks ago. If he's been doing that the whole time, why haven't the rest of us fallen?"

"I don't know. Maybe it wasn't for the tribe. Maybe he was using them to possess animals like those wolves. He could have a completely different plan for the tribe. Still, we probably shouldn't leave this just lying around. Give me a second."

Jez sank his power into the ground. Water from the lake permeated the soil. Whether it was because he'd bonded with the lake when he'd stepped into it or because the soil diluted the effects of the water, it only gave the slightest resistance to his touch, and he brought its power to the surface. It interrupted the energy of the circle. All the runes flared to life at once before leaving blackened remains. The runes themselves were still there, but they were no longer capable of maintaining the energy for a circle.

"That's good enough." Jez turned to Galine. "Let's go back to the town."

They started walking but Aniel just stared out over the lake and didn't follow. The four of them exchanged glances and Galine approached the pharim lord.

"My lord, will you come with us?" Aniel just cocked his head and Galine looked over his shoulder at Jez. "We can't exactly force him."

Jez stood directly in front of Aniel, and his snake like eyes focused on Jez. "Aniel." A sound like a purr rose from his throat, and Jez glanced at Galine. "He seems to respond to his name."

Jez beckoned and started to walk away. Aniel stared at him for a few seconds. He shot one last look over the lake before following. Jez waited for Galine to take the lead. Beside him, Osmund chuckled.

"What?" Jez asked.

Osmund looked back toward Aniel. The pharim could take one step for every two of theirs and so he frequently stopped a few seconds to look around.

"You realize you've got the high lord of the Beastwalkers following you like a trained dog, right?" Osmund asked.

Galine glared at him, but Lina just laughed out loud.

CHAPTER 33

Jez wiped sweat from his brow and silently cursed the sun, which seemed to have turned the jungle into an oven. In the day it had taken them to make back, Lina had tried using mental magic to restore Aniel. The effort had left her screaming in pain for half an hour, and they had abandoned the effort.

"The jungle seems quiet," Jez said as they neared the town.

"They're wondering what Aniel is doing with us," Galine said, seemingly indifferent to the heat.

Jez took in the jungle around them. Even the trees seemed to rustle less than they should in the wind.

"Everything?"

Galine grinned. "He is a high lord of the pharim."

Jez nodded. "Fair enough. Have we been spotted? I haven't seen anyone."

Galine stopped and stared at him for a second before snorting and continuing on. "I don't know what I find more unbelievable, that you didn't see the doe an hour and a half ago or that you actually think you could approach a town of my kind without being seen."

Jez inclined his head in concession. A few more minutes of travel proved Galine correct. They came into the clearing, and Jez gaped.

He'd assumed there would be the few dozen beast men he'd seen the last time they were here, but there were hundreds gathered here, of nearly every animal Jez had ever imagined and more than a few he had never dreamed of. Some were almost completely beast save for a few features. One horse with a peculiar set of human eyes sent chills down Jez's spine whenever he looked into them. Others, like the bird woman he'd seen earlier, had only one or two animal traits. The vast majority were somewhere in between. There was even a woman covered in fish scales who had webbed feet and hands.

"How many are there?"

Galine shrugged. "We don't really keep count."

"They can't all live in this town."

"There are a few, smaller settlements scattered throughout the valley. This is the largest, or at least the old city was. Most of our people live out in the wild, though. The towns are only for those of us who maintain closer ties to humanity than to the beast."

Jez raised an eyebrow. "So Welb was right about you?"

Galine shook his head. "Welb thinks I neglect the beast entirely. I think the opposite of him. We were never intended to choose one side over the other."

Jez eyed the crowd. "What are they waiting for?"

"Him."

Galine glanced back at Aniel. The pharim lord's eyes scanned the gathered beast men before looking back at Jez and letting out that strange half purr. The beast men murmured to each other as Jez returned Aniel's stare, unsure of what else to do.

"Do you want to tell everyone at once, Galine?" Lina asked. "Is there a town council, or something?"

Galine inclined his head. He uttered several syllables that were closer to growls than words, and half a dozen beast men came out of the crowd. Galine nodded to a large hut and motioned for Jez to follow. The building had a dirt floor and a thatched roof. The walls were made of some sort of clay and a single window let in the sunlight as well as a soft breeze. Slowly, the people Galine had called entered.

There was a woman with a face like a lizard who was covered in scales. The person next to her, Jez couldn't tell if it was a man or a woman, had leathery grey skin and a nose that nearly went down to their waist. Ravous was there, as well as a large black bird with a woman's face. A man with the body of a horse had to duck his head to come in. The last one to enter was Welb. The wolf man stood in the doorway for a long time. He looked back at his companions. Grita still looked unsure of herself, but the others motioned him forward. Still Jez wondered if he was going to enter. When Aniel looked at Welb, he shrank back a little before clenching his teeth and forcing himself forward.

They all stood with their backs straight and looked the pharim lord in the eye. Aniel examined them all. He sniffed at the grey skinned man, but otherwise he didn't acknowledge them.

"Lord Aniel?"

Welb's voice was much quieter than it had been before. He kept looking over his shoulder as if he was afraid, though Jez told himself that couldn't be it. Aniel looked at Welb, but his gaze only lingered on the wolf man for a few seconds before turning away. He started to examine the black bird, but the others focused on Galine. Welb showed his teeth.

"Galine, what did you do to him?"

Galine just stared at him. Then, he laughed. His mane shook as his head rocked back and forth. Welb's fur bristled, and the other beast men didn't seem to know how to react. Finally Galine regained his composure.

"Welb, what do you think I could do to Aniel himself?"

Welb growled, but didn't respond. Mummers of affirmation came from the others. The horse man approached and laid a hand on Aniel's shoulder. The lord of the Beastwalkers cocked his head but otherwise did nothing.

"What happened?" The crow's voice was so much like a caw that her words could barely be understood.

"We're still trying to figure that out, Krita. It seems the speaking stone was also a focusing crystal capable of drawing on Aniel's power. A mage got ahold of it. We think he used it against Aniel, though I don't know what he did."

"A mage?" Ravous asked, his single eye widening. "A human mage did this to Lord Aniel?"

"Not just a mage," Jez said. "A demon in human flesh. He was the same one who summoned the demon that possessed you."

Ravous hissed, his forked tongue tasting the air. "What do we do?"

Galine looked like he was going to say something, but instead he gave Jez a hard look. Jez wanted to take a step back, but he held his ground. To his surprise, Galine inclined his head. Silence followed as everyone understood the implication. Galine was giving Jez authority. Ravous grinned and inclined his head as well. Welb snarled, but the rest just looked at Jez.

"Can you search the valley?" Jez asked

Ravous nodded. "Yes, we can search through the entire area in a day."

"Ravous..." Galine began.

"We are of Aniel," Ravous said. "Nothing can remain hidden if we wish to find it."

Jez nodded and gave them a quick description of Sharim. "Find him, but don't attack him. Come back to find me."

"What can you do that we cannot?" Welb asked.

Jez was about to answer when Ravous put a hand on Welb's shoulder. Welb looked at the snake man.

"It's not what we can do." Ravous said. "It's what can be done to us. If this mage turns Aniel's power against us, there is nothing we will be able to do."

CHAPTER 34

The beast men went out from the town in a rush. They flew through the air and ran on the ground. They burrowed in the earth and swam in the streams. Even Toden joined the search. Jez wanted to go with one of the search parties, but the others convinced him to stay in town. It wouldn't do any good if Sharim were found while Jez was out in the jungle with no one knowing where he was.

Jez paced back and forth in the council house. He and his friends had decided to take shelter from the sun while the others searched. Lina and Osmund were leaning against a wall, and Galine, though unbothered by the heat, had joined them and stood near the door.

"You don't think they can do it in a day?" Jez asked.

Galine shook his head. "It's possible, but I doubt it. We've never searched the entire valley, and for all Ravous's confidence, he has no idea what that entails. It could be a long time, maybe even days or weeks."

"That's a lot longer than I would've hoped."

Galine shrugged. "Ravous overestimates us. There is no part of the valley that they couldn't reach in a day, but that's not the same thing as a systematic search. Sharim could've already left the valley, and we'd have no way of knowing."

"No, I don't think so. He's had plenty of time before now to leave if that was what he wanted."

"Before now, we didn't have a trio of powerful mages on our side. He could be afraid of you."

"But aren't you all mages?" Lina asked. "You bound our power when we first met."

Galine smiled. "You have no idea how hard that was. We almost retreated when we realized all three of you were mages. It's extremely difficult to work any magic outside of the dominion of beasts, and many of us have forsaken even that."

"Why?"

Galine shivered and walked to the window. He stared into the town for a few seconds before turning to Jez. "It's uncomfortable to use. Perhaps it reminds us, on some level, of what we left behind when we were human."

"I hate just waiting here," Jez said. "Isn't there anything we can do?"

"Perhaps. Lord Aniel was able to find Sharim before. He might, at least, point us in the right direction."

"Do you know how we get him to understand what we want?"

"Maybe we don't need to," Galine said. "We didn't last time."

"I thought the whole point in bringing him here was to keep him out of danger," Lina said.

"We don't need to follow him to Sharim," Galine said. "We just need an indication of where he is."

He walked through the door and into town. Aniel had been left to wander the center of the settlement. A group of Welb's wolves, including Grita, stayed near him, ensuring he'd be safe, though he seemed not to notice them. He was apparently content to examine all

the dwellings in the town, though as soon as Jez neared, Aniel looked to him.

"Aniel," Jez said. "Do you know where Sharim is?" Aniel cocked his head, not seeming to understand. Jez let out a breath. "The one who did this to you. The one who shouldn't be here."

Aniel inclined his head and took a step. By the time his foot hit the ground, he had transformed into a sleek black panther. He looked over at Jez and let out a low rumble and bounded into the trees, leaving his minders stunned. Some of the wolves followed him into the trees. Jez took off after them, followed closely by his friends, but by the time they'd reached the tree line, Jez was afraid he'd lost the trail. He went into the woods blindly. After a few minutes, another roar made him look up. Aniel was in the trees, his golden eyes gleaming.

Strangely, Jez realized he could hear the wolves moving through the woods behind them, and he suspected it was Aniel's doing. None of them sounded close. As soon as Jez stood under Aniel's tree, the pharim lord leapt to another one. It went on like that for nearly an hour, and the wolves fell farther and farther behind.

Eventually, they came to an isolated stream. A red-tailed hawk swooped down and landed on a rock. Aniel's eyes locked onto Jez and his friends, somehow conveying that they should be silent. They watched as the hawk's form writhed and transformed into that of Welb. The wolf man bent down and started lapping up water from the stream. Aniel jumped from his branch and landed a few feet away from him. Welb looked up and growled but stopped when he saw it was only an animal.

"I don't suppose you've seen this demon, have you?" Welb asked the panther.

The panther cocked his head in a very familiar gesture. Welb's eyes went wide, and Aniel's body became liquid and flowed into his familiar shape, with six wings and curved horns.

"L...Lord Aniel."

"How?" Galine said as he stepped out of the trees. Welb looked from Galine to Aniel. He showed his teeth in an expression of shock. He coiled his leg muscles as if preparing to strike. It was with a visible effort that he calmed down.

"I've been practicing," Welb said. "It's not so hard to do it again once you get the hang of it."

"He's lying," Lina said.

"Are you sure?" Jez asked.

Lina narrowed her eyes. "I did spend all of my life learning the politics of the nations. I know when someone is lying to me."

"She does have a point, Welb," Galine said. "It was a lie and a clumsy one at that. What are you really doing here? Why is it that you can change?"

Welb looked from Galine to Aniel before letting out a breath. He opened his mouth to speak, but at a glance from the pharim lord, he sighed.

"I can change because I was never forced into this form."

For a while, they all just stared at him. Lina understood first.

"You never came under the influence of a beast mind."

"No."

"You were worried about Aniel seeing you. You thought he would know what you are." Welb hesitated for a second before nodding.

"You're a mage?" Galine asked. "Why would you hide that? It rarely happens, but we've had mages who tired of human life join us before."

Welb's head bobbed. "Yes, I...I was embarrassed that I had not left my human side behind."

Lina pursed her lips and shook her head. "You're lying again."

"What? No, I'm not."

"You were ready to attack Galine for being too human. Do you really expect us to believe you couldn't stay in wolf shape for a few weeks?"

"Don't judge him too harshly," Galine said as he moved to stand beside Welb. "To fall under the influence of the beast mind is essentially to die. It's not such an easy thing to do."

"Yes." Welb latched onto the excuse. "That's it."

He responded just a little too quickly, and his words sounded hollow. An idea began to form in Jez's mind, and he walked up to Welb. "You don't like humans very much, do you?"

"I've been in your cities before. I find nothing appealing about them."

"And the Keep of the Hosts?"

Welb's eyes widened for a second. If Jez hadn't been looking for it, he would've missed it. A heartbeat later, Welb was shaking his head. Before he had a chance to speak, Jez drew his sword and delivered a quick slash. Welb jumped back and snarled. He raised his claws, but Jez had already put his sword away. Green motes of light bled from his wound. The wolf man looked down, and the light changed into blood, but seeing that the deception was pointless, he allowed the blood to returned to motes of light a second later.

"You're a Beastwalker," Galine said.

Jez shook his head. "If he were a Beastwalker, he wouldn't have been afraid to see Aniel. I think he was a Beastwalker, a long time ago. You're an afur, aren't you?" Welb started to shake his head, but Jez cut him off. "Did you rebel because you hate humans so much?"

"Because you think yourself so superior," he spat.

His words silenced everyone. Even Jez took a step back. Welb's teeth seemed to sharpen, and his eyes focused on Jez. Osmund moved to his side, embers flickering around his fingers, but Welb's outrage only lasted a second. Then his shoulders slumped and he lowered his head.

"We were set to watch over the world and given power to do so, and the one thing, above all else that we had to respect, was mortal choice. Human choice. On top of that, humans were given power over the beasts."

"Humans were also given power over other humans," Jez said. "It's how Sharim took control of the king."

Welb shook his head. "That's different. I'm not talking about crafting a working to force your will upon another being. Even beast magic doesn't allow one to do that. I am talking about claiming one being as your own to do with as you will, with no one having the right to say otherwise."

"Some human kingdoms keep slaves," Jez said.

"And yet in few is a slaver thought highly of. In many, they are considered evil men. Who would think the same of a farmer with his horses? You take the wool of sheep for your clothes and slaughter cattle for food. You keep birds in cages. Even your insults reflect it. If someone is messy, you call them a pig. If they simply follow others and make no choices of their own, you call them a dog."

Jez glanced at Osmund, remembering when he'd said that very thing about Aniel. The larger boy loosened his collar, and Lina glared at him.

"Because of that, you rebelled?" Galine asked.

"You make it sound so petty."

"Wasn't it?"

"You don't understand. My task was to watch over the beasts. If a Lifegiver's charge was fed a poison drink, the Lifegiver could heal him. If a human tried to free a demon watched over by a Shadowguard, the Shadowguard could interfere." A chill ran down Jez's spine, but Welb went on. He knelt down and allowed a lizard to crawl on his hand. It looked up at him and hissed before plopping back on the ground. "But if a human claimed an animal I was watching over, I could do nothing. It was my whole reason for being, and I was powerless to prevent it. Of course I rebelled." He practically shouted the word. In the distance, a wolf howled. "How could I do anything else?"

"Are you working with Sharim?" Jez held his hand at his side, ready to summon his crystal sword.

"What? No, of course not."

"You rebelled against Aniel and the Creator before."

"In order to fulfill my task., not to create animals possessed by demons. Though he may banish me from this valley, I want Aniel restored as much as anyone."

Jez looked at Lina. She stared at Welb for several seconds before nodding. "I think he's telling the truth."

"Galine?"

"I don't know. I'm not sure how much I trust one who lied about what he is. We are the children of Aniel."

"So was I," Welb said. "Once. I simply wish to be one again."

"We do not hate humans."

"You don't interact with them. Does my dislike of their kind really matter if I'll never see one?"

Galine raised an eyebrow. "Is that why your challenges always felt so half-hearted?"

"You must deal with the beast masters of the Carceri Academy. They maintain kennels and stables, and yet they are highly respected. You must treat them with honor. I want no part in that."

Jez glanced at Galine. "What do you think?"

"He's been here for longer than I have, and Lord Aniel must've intended something for him. He did lead us here."

"Aniel whose mind is gone," Lina said.

"He led us to Sharim as well," Galine said. "Perhaps Welb could be useful."

Jez's eyes went from Welb to Galine. He didn't trust the wolf man, but Aniel walked up to him and put a hand on his shoulder and smiled. Jez nodded just as a man with hawk wings landed a few feet away. His eyes flicked to Aniel, and he inclined his head before he looked to Galine.

"Vulen, what is it?" Galine asked.

"We found him."

CHAPTER 35

Vulen flew overhead, circling several times to allow Jez and his companions to keep up. He led them to a small cave near a stream that was fed by the lake. A flock of bird men had perched in the surrounding trees to watch, and according to them, Sharim had gone into the cave a while ago but hadn't come out.

"Is there another entrance?" Jez asked.

"We don't have every cave mapped out," Galine said. "There could be. There is a rather extensive network of tunnels under the valley."

Osmund put a hand on Jez's shoulder. "You know this could be a trap."

Jez nodded and summoned his sword. He drew more deeply of Luntayary's power than he normally did, and his flesh started to burn. He could almost imagine smoke rising from his skin. If he kept this up too long, it could damage him permanently, but he didn't want to take any chances, not where Sharim was concerned.

"Osmund, you should stay here."

"You could need my help."

"You won't be much help if Sharim takes control of you."

"You can transform too," Osmund said. "How do you know he won't be able to do the same to you?"

"I don't think it's the same thing. If he could have, he would have last time."

"Jez, if Osmund is right..." Galine paused.

"Then, I'll have Lina with me to free me like she did for Osmund."

"I'm coming with you?" Lina's face had gone a little pale.

"We already know you can counter Sharim's mental magic."

Lina shook her head. "Jez, he just planted a suggestion to attack Aniel in Osmund's mind. By the time I got to him, Sharim wasn't actively influencing him. I just undid what he had done, but if I go against him when he's actually trying, I'll lose"

"Fine," Jez said without taking his eyes from the cave. "If I come flying out of there, do what you need to do."

"You're going to leave me?"

Jez threw up his hands in frustration and glared at her. "You just said you wanted to stay."

"No, I didn't. I said I can't stand against him directly. That doesn't mean I won't go."

Jez let out a long breath. "Look, I think it would help to have you along, but I'm not going to force you to come. It's up to you, but I'm leaving now."

Jez turned away and started walking toward the cave. Dried leaves crunched as he stepped onto them. A second later, leaves rustled beside him, and he smiled.

"I'm glad to have you along," he said without turning around.

"Well, you're hopeless without me," Lina's voice said from behind her illusion. "Do you want me to hide you too?"

Jez shook his head. "It makes everything a little dim."

"That's because I'm bending light around you. Enough of it gets through that you should barely notice."

"I do barely notice, but right now, I want to be as alert as possible. If it looks like I'm getting into trouble, hide me."

"But Jez, you're always getting into trouble."

"Don't roll your eyes at me."

"You can't even see me."

"It doesn't matter. I know you were doing it."

The friendly banter calmed his nerves a little, and his racing heart slowed. He crouched in a bush near the entrance and tried to look inside, but it just looked like an ordinary cave. He didn't even smell sulfur.

"I'm about to charge in." His voice was pitched low, and he hoped the noise of the jungle drifting in from behind would swallow his words. "Come in right after me. Watch out for wards against illusions."

Lina didn't answer, but Jez could imagine her nodding. He took several deep breaths to calm his thoughts, but it did little good. His heart was racing as he scanned for movement, but everything was still.

"Do you sense anything?" Lina asked.

Jez breathed deeply, but didn't catch so much as a hint of sulfur. He wove a ward against illusion to banish any working Sharim might have left in place. He'd grown familiar enough with Lina's power to be able to recognize her working and omit her, but illusions done by anyone else should've been dispelled. Nothing happened. Either these were done in a way he couldn't detect, or there was nothing here to find.

"Let's try deeper into the cave," Jez said.

He didn't wait for a response before entering. It wasn't long before they'd gone too deep for the light from outside to be any help. Lina summoned a ball of light so they could see, though she kept it dim. Jez hoped it would go unseen. The cave went on for a long time, and though they tried to walk softly, their footsteps seemed to echo forever. Every once in a while, Jez thought he heard something and turned in its direction with his sword raised, but he never saw anything. Eventually, the passage opened up to a wide cavern that had two ways out apart from the way they'd come in.

"I have no idea which way to go," Jez said.

"There's something here," Lina said. "Dispel the illusions."

Jez nodded and complied. The ground rippled and blackened marks appeared on the stone, though Lina's working didn't provide enough illumination for him to see in any details. Jez looked toward the light. "Can you make that brighter?"

The light intensified, and a circle of burned out runes came into view. Jez knelt down and ran his fingers across the ground, but he felt no hum of power. This circle was similar to the makeshift one he'd used in his failed attempt to summon a Beastwalker, though many of the patterns were much more complex. Near one edge of the circle, lines curved around an empty space just large enough to accommodate the focusing crystal. He'd seen something like this before, in the circle Sharim had used to summon the demon Maries.

"Well, it's a permanent summoning, but that's not too surprising."

He looked closer at the runes for the focusing crystal. There was more to it than the other of its kind he'd seen. Lina appeared next to him causing him to jump. He glared at her, and she rolled her eyes.

"There's no one else here." She pointed at set of eight concentric circles. "What are all those?"

"It looks almost like the universal symbol, the one that represents everything, but that's only seven circles." Jez touched the outer one.

"This circle is a little different. It feels like it's been carved deeper."

"What does that mean?"

"Normally nothing. Most of the time, more depth to a symbol done accidently." He paused. "Generally, it would actually weaken the circle."

"I don't think that's what happened here," Lina said.

Jez raised an eyebrow. "When did you become an expert on summoning?"

"I'm not, but Sharim made this circle. Do you really think he would accidently weaken it?"

Jez sighed. "Probably not."

"So what does it mean if it's not an accident?"

"It's emphasis." Jez closed his eyes as he tried to remember how different runes interacted with each other. This wasn't a standard rune, and he'd never been particularly gifted at discerning specialized ones. "All of everything, maybe. Everything completely?"

She walked a few feet away and pointed to a rune made of a tooth and claw, the image representing the Beastwalkers. "It's connected to this one."

"No it's not."

She rolled her eyes. "Not in any way you can see, but there were runes in the air too."

"You can see those?"

She kept her eyes focused on the area just above the ground. "Master Kerag has been working with me on it. Runes are almost like illusions. At least they're close enough. There's a working he taught me. It's not perfect, and if there's a lot of other light in the area, the images can be corrupted, but since we're in a cave..."

She closed her eyes. A second later, flickering yellow light appeared from the runes on the floor. Other dimmer images popped into existence in the air forming a dome of distorted runes. They were blurry, and several of them were missing key lines. Still, it looked even more like the circle Sharim had used in Rumar. There were a few significant differences, though. As Lina had said, a curved line arced from the concentric circles and connected them to the rune of the Beastwalkers. The realization hit him like a hammer.

"All the Beastwalkers." Jez's voice was barely above a whisper. "He was trying to summon all of them."

He examined the outer circle again. Several thin lines connected it to four other runes that represented the four elements. Those four points, in turn, connected to each other in a complex web that he doubted he could've crafted if he tried for a year. Even as he spoke, he couldn't believe what he was saying.

"He wanted to summon them completely into this world to bring all their power here."

"Why? Wouldn't that just make them more able to stop him?"

Jez's mouth had gone dry. "That will make them able to be killed, but he couldn't do it. Not entirely. He doesn't have enough power."

"But he has Aniel's focusing crystal."

"A focusing crystal doesn't work like that. It doesn't actually give you more power. It just helps you direct it to get more from the power you have."

"Isn't that basically the same thing?"

"Kind of, but not really." He stared into her light, trying to think of a way to explain it. "It's like if instead of making a really big illusion of a monster, you made two really small illusions of the monster and put them in front of someone's eyes. To them it would be the same thing, but you would only use a fraction of the power."

Lina nodded in understanding. "And he can't use that to summon a Beastwalker?"

"Maybe one. That's probably what happened to Talos, but every Beastwalker in the Keep of the Hosts? He doesn't have nearly enough power for that, no matter how good his control is."

"We are in a place of power, Jez."

"But the lake is outside."

"Why didn't he do it out there then?"

Jez waved at the walls. Some of the runes glowed on the rocks. "He had more control here. Runes made in living things like trees are less potent. Runes made in the air won't survive without power being poured into them."

"Well then, where did he think he was going to get the power to make this work?"

Jez thought about that for a second before nodding. "You're right. We're missing something. Give me a second. Let me see if I can figure this out. How much longer can you keep it up?"

She smirked. "Probably longer than you can stay awake."

He cocked his head. "I'm not sleepy."

She let out a breath and rolled her eyes. "I know that. I can keep it up as long as you need it."

Jez felt his face heat up but nodded. He moved through the circle slowly, trying to understand exactly how it worked. Eventually, he reached the rune of water. Several strands of power connected it to a web linking it to the other elements. A final strand connected it to the concentric circles. He was about to move on when he noticed one of the strands went directly to the earth symbol without passing through the web in between. It came out of the top of the water rune and went into the bottom of the earth rune, and it seemed to be pulsing slightly.

"I think there's something missing here."

"Probably," Lina said. "Like I said, this isn't perfect. What's missing?"

That rune combination could mean something about drawing water from the earth. He nodded. That made sense. "Hold on."

She sniffed, but he'd already closed his eyes. There were several streams that were fed by the lake. It wasn't impossible that some of those streams ran beneath the valley. He sank his senses into the earth. The stones thrummed with power. It wasn't a lot, just enough to set his senses buzzing. As he went deeper, though, the power increased. Twenty feet down, he was nearing the limits of his abilities. The stones were practically alive with energy. His consciousness pressed against a vein of energy that seemed to resist his efforts to probe it. He took a deep breath and drew back.

"There's an underground spring that comes from the lake."

"Could Sharim have used that to call all the Beastwalkers?"

"Not by itself, but with Aniel's speaking stone?" He shook his head. "I don't know. I don't think so. There's something else, though."

"What?"

"If Sharim called all the Beastwalkers into this world, where are they?"

CHAPTER 36

They went into one of the passages leading out of the cavern, but before long, they reached a dead end. The other one split three ways after a few hundred yards. Unwilling to risk getting lost, they returned to the cave entrance and Jez dismissed his sword. Osmund was waiting just outside. When he saw them, he tensed his muscles, and his hand went to his sword. Jez raised his hands.

"Calm down. He's not in control of me," Jez said. Osmund hesitated for a second before letting his hands drop away from his weapon. Jez let out a breath of relief. "It looks like he escaped through some underground passages."

They quickly related what they had found. Galine showed his teeth and let out a snarl, but Welb looked worried.

"That explains it."

"Explains what?"

"Aniel. Probably the rest of them too. When I was cast from the Keep of the Hosts, it was a strain on my mind." He let out a bark. "Strain is an understatement. It broke me. It didn't happen to the other pharim orders, but the change was too much for our dual natures. I spent a century wandering the world as a wolf. I think I changed a couple of times, but it's hard to remember."

"But Aniel isn't fully in this world," Jez said. "At least I don't think he is."

"No, you're right, but he's most of the way here." He growled and eyed Aniel. "I should've seen it before. It's the same thing that happened to us."

"Aniel was a shark before we found him."

"The rest of them could be wandering the valley." Welb brushed at a fly buzzing around his face. "For all we know, that could be one of them."

"Is it?" Galine asked.

Welb's eyes flickered green for a second before shaking his head. "No, there are no transformed beings nearby."

"How many of you can do that?" Jez asked. "Detect transformation, I mean."

"Not many," Galine said. "As I said, most of us put magic of any kind away. Your friend Mirous can, as well as Rouwglar."

"Who?"

Galine huffed. "Toden and Grita. You must accept that they are new people now. They haven't been here long enough for their abilities to atrophy. There are a few others who maintain the ability. Most came within the past decade or so."

"We need to contact them. If we tell them what to look for, they might be able to find others."

"Assuming Sharim doesn't already have them."

"If Sharim had them, they'd already be dead," Jez said. "If that's the case, we can't help them."

"That doesn't exactly make me feel better." Galine looked up to the branches. "Vulen, find those you can in the valley. We'll return to town and get the rest."

Vulen nodded, and her flock took to the air. Welb watched them go before he shifted into the form of a hawk.

"I'll meet you in town." With his mouth shaped the way it was, there was no way Welb should've been able to speak, but somehow, he did, though his voice had that same squawking quality that the other bird men possessed. "The sooner we get started, the better."

Galine nodded, and Welb took off. They went back to the town the same way they had come. Since they didn't have to cut a new trail, they travelled a lot faster than they had before. They moved in silence, but Jez couldn't help but wonder if every animal he saw was actually a Beastwalker. As they neared the town, the animals stopped appearing. Galine obviously noticed too, and he kept looking into the trees.

"What is it?" Lina asked.

"There are no animals," Jez said. His nose wrinkled as he caught the scent of sulfur. Instantly, his crystal sword was in his hand. "There are demons nearby."

Osmund sniffed. "No, I smell it too. That's not demons. That's a fire."

"There," Galine said as he pointed through the trees.

A column of dark smoke rose in the distance, and the air around it shimmered as it was distorted by the heat. It was difficult to tell through the trees, but Jez thought it might be...

"The town is on fire," Galine said. "Catch up when you can. I'm needed."

Without waiting for a response, Galine disappeared into the trees.

CHAPTER 37

It took Jez and his friends nearly half an hour to reach the town. The clearing was little more than a blackened field. The huts had been reduced to ash and most of the nearby trees had been torn down. Several partially-human forms lay unmoving on the ground, and Galine was pulling up a burned log to rescue the snake man who was trapped beneath.

Welb was running back and forth pulling beast men out of the rubble. Jez only hesitated for a second before drawing water out of the air and using it to extinguish the few fires that still burned. That released a cloud of smoke that made Jez cough for a few seconds before it cleared. Osmund moved to help Galine, and Lina started digging into ruined buildings to see if she could help anyone.

Jez lost track of how long they worked to find and help the wounded. Most of those who could be saved had already been extracted from the rubble, but there were still a few left. Jez had been using his sense of earth and water to find survivors. A few had only a broken arm or leg, but most couldn't even stand. Jez located a dozen, but it still felt like far too few.

The injured were laid out in a row at one side of the clearing while others tended to them. The sun had nearly disappeared in the west when Welb, once again in the form of a wolf man, walked up next to him. Jez was still searching, but he hadn't found anyone in a while.

"We think that's everyone."

"What's happened?"

"Sharim came with fifty beast men." Welb glared at Jez, who took an involuntary step back. "We could've held him back if most of our people hadn't been out looking for him. As it was, he tore through the town practically unopposed. On his way out, he called fire down from the sky."

"How many did he take prisoner?" Jez asked.

"One." The word was practically a growl.

"What?"

"He only took one."

"But that doesn't make sense. He crafted a summoning circle to call lotheen specifically to possess you."

"A circle you destroyed."

"That wouldn't be any more than a minor inconvenience to him. He could craft another one. It would just take a little time."

"Why would he attack at all?" Lina asked. "He didn't when he possessed most of the beast men last time. Why is this different?"

"Maybe you're just wrong about what he's doing," Welb said. "Or maybe you lied to us to get us away from town."

Jez blinked at him. "Why would you think that?"

Welb spread his arms in a gesture that encompassed the ruins of the town. "If not for you, we would've been able to defend ourselves."

"Who was taken?" Lina asked.

"Who do you think? He used that stone to catch Aniel. Because of you, a demon now has a high lord of the pharim as a captive."

"That's enough, Welb."

Galine's voice cracked from the other side of the clearing. In the space of a few heartbeats, the lion man had crossed the clearing and was looking down at Welb, a low rumble rising from his chest.

"No, it's not nearly enough. Because you're too human, you've led our tribe to the brink of destruction."

"You hate humans too much." Galine said. Welb growled, but Galine smirked. "You've challenged me before, Welb. You did it a few days ago. It didn't turn out well for you."

"You can't really believe I was trying. I've spent lifetimes hiding among you, but if I fought to my full ability, you wouldn't stand a chance. I've been avoiding it because I didn't want to be discovered by Aniel, but if that's what it takes to get him back, I might just do it."

"I met an afur once," Lina said. Every eye turned to her, but rather than trying to avoid their stares as Jez might have, she stood up straight, and her hair and clothes began to shimmer.

Welb snorted. "Stop lying, girl. You don't do it well."

She smiled. "Actually, I'm very good at it, but that's beside the point. She'd been a Veilspeaker once. She went by the name of Villia, and she was an advisor to King Haziel. Just like you, she wanted to reclaim part of her purpose so she hid in Rumar Keep."

Welb shook his head. "If that were true, she would've been discovered."

"Like you were discovered hiding among the beast men?" She wrinkled her brow. "I don't think the pharim high lords really care what you do as long as you stay out of their way."

"What would a human know of these things?" He stood taller and showed his teeth. "What would a human know about any of this?"

Lina was about to respond, but Jez stepped forward. There was only one way Welb was going to listen. He drew deeply of

Luntayary's power. His flesh began to burn as wings emerged from his back, and his clothes transformed to sapphire robes. He met Welb's eyes. The wolf man flinched, and suddenly, he didn't seem so intimidating. Jez inclined his head and released the power, returning back to his human form. Standing was difficult, but he didn't think it would be good to show weakness so he forced himself to stand up straight.

"You're an afur too," Welb said.

Jez shook his head. "I never rebelled."

"You're..." Welb took a deep breath. "You're a pharim? No, that doesn't make sense. You're no Beastwalker. Those robes were those of a Shadowguard, and no pharim can interfere in the business of another order."

"Are you turning away my help?"

Welb's muscles tensed, and he bent his legs and looked like he was prepared to leap. Jez took a step back and raised his hands.

"I would welcome help from a true pharim, but even if I believed a Shadowguard had somehow gotten around the limitation barring them from helping, I can smell your burned flesh. You're no pharim."

Jez cleared his throat. "It's a little complicated."

Welb huffed out a breath. "Another way to say it's a lie. I think you should leave. We'll recover our lord ourselves."

Galine glared at him. "You do not speak for the tribe, Welb, whatever you may think."

Welb leapt in much the same way he'd done the first time Jez had seen him. Once again, Galine moved to grab his neck, but Welb's hands flashed, and he knocked aside Galine's arm, leaving three gashes in the lion's arm. Welb crashed into him, and though he was much smaller than Galine, the lion man was forced back a few steps.

He jerked his head to the left, barely avoiding Welb's jaws. Galine's paws shot forward, but Welb twisted out of the way with an almost casual ease as he slashed at Galine's chest. Galine tried to back up to avoid the strike, but Welb was too fast. The wolf's clawed hands moved in a blur, and two other gashes formed on Galine's chest.

The lion man roared and surged forward, but Welb sidestepped him before jumping into the air. He landed on Galine's back, and his jaws closed around his neck. Galine froze. All the beast men in town were staring. A thin trickle of blood ran down Galine's neck and Welb released. He jumped from Galine's back and slowly walked in front of him.

"You are beaten. I lead the tribe now."

Galine inclined his head. He was breathing heavily. "So you do."

Welb pointed at Jez. "He and his friends will leave. They are no longer welcome here."

Galine nodded and turned to Jez. "Let's go."

"You're going with them?" Welb looked surprised.

"Of course. Your leadership may well lead the tribe into destruction. These humans are the only chance we have. I only wish you could see that."

CHAPTER 38

What do we do now?" Jez asked.

They were a couple of miles away from the town. Every time an animal stopped to look at them, Jez wondered if it was an imprisoned Beastwalker, but none of them had a good enough sense of beast magic to tell for sure.

"Where would Sharim complete his ritual?"

"Wouldn't it be back in the cave?" Lina asked.

Galine shook his head. "He can't use a ruined circle."

Jez and Lina exchanged glances, and Jez let out a forced laugh. Galine raised an eyebrow. Jez winced. "We were in a hurry to find Sharim."

"You can't mean you left the circle intact."

"Look, it obviously wasn't my best decision, but at least we know where to look."

"We don't have the time we would have had, if he had to craft an entirely new one," Galine said.

Jez rolled his eyes and started walking away. "You can stay here and keep complaining, or you can come help. We still have some time. He needs to alter it if it's going to affect someone as powerful as Aniel."

"Jez," Osmund said as he caught up.

"We don't have time to point fingers. This is Sharim, Osmund."

"I know. I get that. It's just—"

"Just what? I should stand there while he insults me?"

"No. It's just that I'm pretty sure the cave is in the other direction."

Jez stopped. "What?"

"You're heading for the edge of the valley." Osmund pointed a rock formation in the distance, barely visible through the trees. "That's the border of the valley there."

Jez looked over his shoulder. Galine and Lina were staring at him. Lina grinned openly. Galine gave him a small smile before turning and walking into the jungle. Jez let out a breath and rushed to follow. He refused to meet Lina's eyes as they walked. It didn't take them long to reach the cave. This time, the smell of sulfur billowed from the cave mouth and almost made Jez gag.

"He's in there."

Osmund looked at Galine. "Should we stay behind?"

Jez shook his head. "We're going to have to take the risk. Sharim already killed one Beastwalker. Maybe he can only bring them fully here one at a time. We can't let him do that to Aniel. If he's there, I'll attack first. Lina, make distractions, whatever it takes to keep him from focusing on Osmund and Galine."

Lina nodded. "What if he takes control of you?"

Jez bit his lower lip. If Sharim could manage it, it would be a very bad thing. Jez was bound to human flesh for as long as he lived, but if he were to be killed, he'd emerge as the Shadowguard Luntayary with full access to all his abilities, and provided he was permitted to interfere in this matter, he thought he'd be more than a match for Sharim. All it would cost was his life. Osmund met his eyes and inclined his head as he touched the hilt of his sword. It was all that needed to be said.

Lina seemed to catch that there was something unsaid between them. She looked from Jez to Osmund and opened her mouth to speak, but Jez gave her a slight shake of his head, and her lips snapped shut.

"What is it?" Galine asked.

"We just came up with a back-up plan. Don't worry."

Galine's brow furled, but he nodded. Jez stepped forward into the cave.

CHAPTER 39

Light pulsed in the distance. Blue flickered to yellow and back to blue as they descended deeper into the earth. Power hummed against Jez's protection sense, and it was an effort not to let it distract him. They reached one of the final bends before Sharim's lair, and Jez summoned his crystal sword. A false image of himself appeared beside him. Next to it stood an image of Osmund and Galine. Jez nodded to Lina. He took a deep breath and charged.

He stopped in his tracks as he ran into a bear ten feet tall.

Its fur was black, and chitinous plates covered its chest and shoulders. Its eyes glowed red, and it snapped at Jez as soon as he came into range. Jez yelped and fell, barely avoiding the creature's massive jaws. As he cried out, several sets of red eyes appeared on the ceiling. In the light of the circle, Jez could see huge bats hanging there.

They screeched so loudly that Jez thought his ears would bleed. Then, they launched themselves toward him. He lifted his sword but before he had a chance to strike, a flaming blade tore one of the creatures out of the air. Jez realized he was holding his breath, half expecting to see an explosion of green motes, but the body fell to the earth as a burned husk. Ziary stood over him, his sword flashing.

There was a roar that drowned out everything else, and Galine practically flew through the air and slammed into the giant bear. Their cries mingled with each other, and the two creatures became a fury of tooth and claw.

Jez got to his feet. His fingers danced in the air. The smoldering remains said these were possessed animals and not demons, and that meant lotheen. A dozen bands of fire shot forth from his hands, trapping the bats. They fell to the ground, squealing in pain. The protection offered by mortal flesh prevented him from banishing them to the abyss, but the working got them out of the way without killing them. His binding, however, passed right through the bear with no effect whatsoever.

"It's not a lotheen!"

Galine grunted. He'd seized the bear from behind and was holding its arms prone. Though the bear was more massive, Galine's four legs gave him an advantage that the possessed creature couldn't quite overcome. The bear managed to get one hand free and turned, slamming its paw into Galine's face. Galine drew back. One of the bear's claws had ripped into his forehead, and the blood was running into his eyes.

"Go get Sharim," he said as he returned the attack. "This will all be for nothing if he succeeds."

Ziary had already rounded the corner, and Jez followed. His knees were still weak from his temporary transformation into Luntayary, and he was forced to draw on the pharim's power to compensate. The power began burning away at him even as it strengthened him. He rounded the corner and found himself looking right into Sharim's eyes.

Sharim's pale skin was colored by the light of the circle, alternating between yellow and blue. His eyes glowed green as he stared at Aniel who was held down in the center of the circle by chains of light. Sharim raised his hand, but Jez was ready and wove a ward against illusions even before Sharim unleashed a working that would've attempted to trap Jez in a vision of Sharim's making. Sharim smiled.

"You've gotten better since the last time I saw you."

Jez took a step forward, keeping his sword between him and Sharim. "And you still like to talk."

"Unless this is a distraction."

Jez's eyes widened as a snake man rose from the shadows and wrapped itself around him before he had a chance to react. It was only then that he noticed Ziary similarly restrained. Jez tried to call water out of the air, but the snakes seemed to trap his power as well as his body. The head of the one trapping him rose, and Jez was forced to meet its gaze. A scar ran across the left side of its face and a milky orb sat where an eye should be.

"Ravous?"

The snake hissed. Its head shot forward as it prepared to sink its curved teeth into Jez. Jez cried out but Sharim's voice cut in.

"Not quite yet."

Ravous froze less than an inch from Jez's face. Out of the corner of his eye, he saw a similar scene with Osmund. Slowly, the snakes drew back, though their grip didn't lessen. The crystal at Sharim's feet glowed as he lifted a hand toward Jez. His skin began to crawl. The runes shone brightly as they drew power from the stream below. Jez felt himself burning, but he closed his eyes in concentration and forced Luntayary's power back.

"Impressive," Sharim said. "Let's see how you do when I bring the full power of a high lord of the pharim against you."

The chains around Aniel shone a bright as the sun. The lord of the Beastwalkers howled. The sound hit Jez like a wave, and the entire cave shook. Ravous shivered, and for a moment, Jez thought the snake man would release him, but its coils tightened a second later.

A green aura appeared around Sharim's hand shining so brilliantly Jez started to look away, but Ravous hissed, and Jez froze. His skin started to burn and steam rose from his exposed flesh. Jez tried to push the Luntayary away, but it was like trying to stop an earthquake, and Sharim's working rolled over his resistance as if it wasn't there. Power swelled inside of him as his clothes transformed into sapphire robes and wings emerged from his back.

At some unspoken command, Ravous released him. Jez tried to move toward Sharim, but his legs refused to obey. Sharim uttered a harsh syllable, and Jez turned toward Ziary. The snake man holding the scion slithered away but Ziary didn't move. Jez raised his sword to cut down his friend. Then, Ziary vanished.

"What?" Sharim called out. Jez managed to turn in his direction just as understanding dawn on Sharim. "Ah yes. Lina."

He waved a hand and Ziary shimmered back into view. Lina yelped as she appeared a few feet away. Jez struggled against the power holding him but to no avail. He could feel his physical body dying, but there was nothing else he could do.

Sharim cried out, but Aniel had already started to rise, and Sharim turned his full attention to the pharim lord. Freed of the control, Jez forced Luntayary back, and he returned to human form. His knees buckled and he fell, his body drained of strength. Ziary fell to one knee, but he was able to rise again a second later, and he moved toward Sharim. Sharim's eyes widened, but he couldn't seem to take any power from his working on Aniel.

Ziary struck, but his sword was rebuffed by the same shield Sharim had used before. Jez tried to summon the energy to dispel it, but he had nothing left. Again and again, Ziary struck. Cracks began to form in the shield, but it wouldn't be fast enough. The circle was pulsing regularly, almost ready to unleash its energy. The focusing crystal at Sharim's feet was like a green sun.

Aniel roared as every rune shone deep blue. Jez's heart felt like he would explode. He clutched at his chest and curled into a fetal position. He saw Ziary doing the same a few feet away. Neither of them was dong as bad as the snake men.

Ravous had coiled into a ball. His cries sounded nothing like a human's and it sent chills down Jez's spine. The others were screaming, their hisses filled the air.

"Jez, what's wrong?" Lina asked.

"Stop him," Jez managed through the pain. "He's doing it now."

He couldn't tell for sure through his blurred vision, but he thought Lina nodded. She stepped away from him. He tried to lift his head to see what she was doing, but he just didn't have the strength. The pain was too much.

"Now you? You're only human."

"How good is your focus, Sharim?" Lina asked. "Can you keep it going if I invade your mind?"

"You can't possibly think you could defeat me there. My mind has existed since before your world came to be."

"Maybe, but I'll bet you weren't trying to command a high lord of the pharim all that time."

Jez managed to sit up. Lina and Sharim were staring at each other. He could feel the power inside of Lina, barely a fraction compared to the torrent inside of Sharim, but most of Sharim's was directed at Aniel, and he didn't have much to spare for the defense of his mind. Still, Sharim was ancient and powerful, and he'd tapped into the stream below in addition to the power he was siphoning off of Aniel.

The tiniest portion of that power could defend against master mages, and while Lina's skills with illusions were impressive, she was only a fledgling mentalist.

Jez clenched his teeth, trying to think of anything he could do to help. The strength of his body had failed. He didn't dare call on Luntayary's power. His own strength was nearly depleted, his eyes locked on to the water rune, the one used to tap into the stream beneath them.

He closed his eyes and reached down with his power. It took him far too long to find the spring. It resisted his attempts to tap into it, but he pushed with everything he had. Beast magic welled into him. It wasn't a lot. His weakened body couldn't hold much right now, but he embraced it and threw it against Sharim, trying to wrest control of the circle from him.

Even with Sharim trying to control Aniel while defending against Lina, Jez's attack was too weak. Sharim chuckled and the runes flared. Lina took advantage of the distraction and power surged inside of her. Sharim's eyes went wide, and the pain in Jez's chest became so intense it blinded him. Sharim cried out, but whatever Lina had done was too late. Jez felt a huge surge of beast magic, the same magic that governed his own transformation, rushing into the world.

CHAPTER 40

The pain receded, and Jez staggered to his feet. He winced as his clothes rubbed against his skin. The forced transformation had left him covered in blisters. Osmund stood, seeming no worse for wear. Lina was breathing heavily, and Sharim was struggling to stand. Ravous writhed nearby. Aniel lay in an unmoving heap in the center of the circle. Osmund met Jez's eyes and nodded before moving to stand over Sharim with his sword drawn. Jez shambled over to Lina.

"What did you do?"

"I couldn't distract him from his main working, but he was doing five at one time, so I picked one of his lesser ones and went after it. It was some sort of protection. As soon as I got through, he doubled over in pain."

Jez nodded. "It hurt everyone who could transform. He must've been protecting himself from it. When you distracted him..." He waved his hand at Sharim who had just noticed Osmund standing over him.

"You fool," Sharim said. "We have to get out of here."

Osmund snorted and pressed his blade against Sharim's chest. "You don't get to talk now."

Sharim looked unblinkingly into Osmund's eyes as he stood. Osmund's muscled tensed, but he allowed Sharim to rise. Once he was on his feet he threw Aniel uneasy glances. The pharim lord was starting to stir, and Sharim's eyes were wide.

"I don't have control of him."

Jez sneered. "You say that like it's a bad thing."

"It is. You just had to interfere, didn't you? You've seen beast mind. Well, right now, it's claimed the lord of the Beastwalkers and all of his children. When he gets up, there won't be a more dangerous place in the entire world than right here."

He took a step toward the entrance and Osmund's sword flashed as it touched his Sharim's neck. "Don't move."

Sharim sneered. "Do it if you're going to. It'll be better than getting ripped apart by him."

Osmund's eyes darted to Aniel.

"No!" Jez cried out.

It was too late. Jez had faced Sharim in combat six months prior, and he'd learned that among Sharim's other talents, he was a master of the blade, one that you couldn't take your eyes off of, not even for a second.

A sword of liquid flame appeared in Sharim's hands. It moved so fast it left a red streak in the air. It sheared through Osmund's steel weapon before the other boy had even realized Sharim was moving. Osmund barely avoided Sharim's thrust. Sharim's sword swung in a wide arc as he took a step forward, completely heedless of the snake man still struggling to rise.

As soon as he stepped near the head, Ravous's eyes shot open, and he surged forward. His jaws closed on Sharim's leg. Sharim cried out and staggered as Osmund swung his broken blade, but Sharim managed to raise his weapon in time to meet his attack. The remnants of Osmund's weapon melted as they impacted Sharim's. Sharim lifted a hand and a blast of wind drove Osmund back. Sharim scooped up the focusing crystal and stared into it for a second. Osmund recovered, and flame sprouted around his fist. He drew back his arm to deliver a punch, but bat-like wings emerged from Sharim's back and curved horns grew from his head. He leapt back, turning in the air. Osmund started after him, but Sharim disappeared around the corner in the space of a few heartbeats.

"I can't transform," Osmund said.

"Forget that," Jez said between heavy breaths. "Come close."

"He's getting away."

"And we can't move as fast. Come closer."

Osmund stared after Sharim for several seconds before nodding. He moved right next to Jez.

"Now what?"

"Lina hide us. All twelve senses if you can manage."

Her eyes went wide. "I don't think I can."

"Fine. The five physical senses and beast." Jez glanced at Aniel and wracked his brain, trying to remember what other areas else the pharim lord might be strong at.

"Healing," Osmund said. "Then, protection and destruction in that order."

"Eight?"

Osmund shrugged. "You can probably ignore touch." Aniel started to rise, and Osmund let out a sharp breath. "We really don't have time."

Lina shook her head but closed her eyes. The cave became a little dark, and the sounds became muted. Aniel struggled to his feet and shifted into the form of a huge back hound, easily the size of a grizzly bear. Its teeth looked like they could crush stone. It sniffed at the air, and Jez found himself holding his breath. Aniel's eyes focused on them, and he growled. Jez could feel the sound reverberating in his chest.

"Lina," he said.

"I don't know. The illusion is up."

"I don't think it's working," Osmund said.

"I can see that."

"You really should fix it."

"I'm not sure what to do."

The hound leapt at them.

CHAPTER 41

All three of them cried out as the hound tore through the air. It landed right in front of them, directly on top of the snake man who'd been slithering unseen on the ground. It hissed and bit into him, but either Aniel was immune to poison or his current form was too large for the amount of venom the snake man injected. Either way, the bite didn't slow him down. He snapped at the snake man's head, but the creature partially withdrew into a thin hole, its body writhing under his paws.

Aniel barked and tried to dig at the rock, but he succeeded in nothing more than inadvertently releasing the hold he had on the snake man, and the rest of it disappeared into the hole. Aniel snapped at the hole, but it had no effect. He turned and scanned the room, but Ravous, the only other snake man who'd been there, was already gone, though Jez hadn't seen him leave. Aniel snorted. He was so close Jez could smell his breath, an earthy scent mingled with the smell of blood.

"Jez, is he supposed to do that?" Lina asked.

"Do what?"

"Breathe."

Jez shook his head. He looked into Aniel's eyes. Though he hoped the pharim lord couldn't see him, Aniel continued to stare forward. He didn't turn away for several seconds. Then, he disappeared down the passage leading to outside. No one moved for a long time. Jez's heart was racing, and he wouldn't have been surprised if the others could hear it. Finally, Lina allowed the illusion to drop.

"By the seven," she said. She let out a laugh. "I guess that was one of the seven, though."

Jez nodded, but a second later, his knees gave way, and he collapsed. The next thing he knew, Osmund was picking him up off the ground.

"What happened?" Lina asked.

Osmund hefted Jez onto his shoulder and started walking. "He was in Luntayary's form too long. He needs a healer. They won't be able to repair the damage, but it might help."

"We're a little far from the Academy."

"Let's go back to the beast men."

"What good will that do?" Lina asked.

"The dominion of beasts is closely related to healing."

"They don't exactly like us."

"They're the best chance we have. We'll just have to hope they're not under the influence of beast mind too."

With an effort, Jez managed to lift his head. Every word was a struggle. "Put me down."

"Nope," Osmund said without slowing.

"I'm fine."

"No you're not."

They rounded the corner, and Osmund stopped. Jez craned his neck and saw Galine lying on top of the massive bear. Both creatures had wounds made by tooth and claw, and blood stained their fur. They were both breathing the regular rhythm of sleep. The bats had vanished. The pain from Aniel's power being bound to the world had probably knocked the combatants out, but both creatures moved as they approached. Lina stepped close to Galine and bent to examine him.

"Don't do that," Osmund said.

She laid a hand on Galine's head. "He's hurt."

"He could be under the influence of beast mind."

She looked over her shoulder at him and glared. "That's even more of a reason to help him. He'd rather be dead than wild like that."

Osmund shook his head. "It was Ravous who said that, not Galine."

"No, Galine just hated the fact that he'd killed."

"Which is why we should get away from here, so he doesn't kill us because he doesn't know he's not supposed to."

She closed her eyes. "One moment."

"Lina, you can't cure beast mind. They've been trying to do that for thousands of years."

She opened one eye and glared at him. "I said one moment."

He sighed and stepped around them. He placed Jez on the ground, and Jez struggled to his feet, though he had to lean against the wall to manage it. Osmund eyed him, but said nothing. Instead, he turned back to Galine and lifted his hands, shrouding them in flame.

"It's not beast mind," she said without opening her eyes. "At least not exactly."

Galine's eyes opened and focused on her. Instinctively, Jez tried to summon his crystal sword, but the effort caused pain to blossom in his chest and sent him to his knees. Osmund glanced down at him, but almost immediately, he returned his attention to Galine. The fire around his hands went from orange to blue, distorting the air around them with heat. Galine started to rise, but Lina's muscles tensed, and to Jez's surprise, she held him down. His eyes glowed purple, and Lina let out a breath. Violet mist came from her mouth and swirled around Galine. He took in a sharp breath, and his eyes dimmed.

"What's going on?" he asked.

Lina withdrew her hand and stood on shaky legs. She backed up and Galine got to his feet. He eyed the bear who was just starting to stir. He looked at Jez.

"I see. Can you help him like you did for the wolves?"

Jez took a step forward and immediately felt like he was going to pass out. He put his hand on the wall to keep his balance and shook his head.

"Then, we should move quickly. I would not want to fight him again."

CHAPTER 42

His mind was buried," Lina said once they'd gotten out of the cave. Jez couldn't move very fast so they were walking slowly. "I just brought it forth."

"So you cured beast mind," Osmund said.

"No, it's not the same thing," Galine said as he ducked under a branch. "When one first comes under the influence of beast mind, it destroys you, leaving only pieces of who you were. That's why it can't be undone. This is different. My mind was still intact. It was just submerged so she could bring me out of it."

Osmund glanced at Jez. "Galine, are there healers in the town?"

"Not in the town, but there are some scattered about the valley. I doubt Welb will be happy if we talk to them. He considers that magic to be too human, but they'll help anyway. Any mind that would hold on to that kind of knowledge would have a hard time turning away any injured. Provided, of course, that any healer we find is lucid."

"I should be able to help if they're not," Lina said.

Galine inclined his head. "Good. Put him on my back."

"What?" Jez asked.

"The three of you move slowly enough as it is. With you injured, you'll be even slower, and we don't have time."

Jez nodded and staggered over to Galine. He tried to use a tree to pull himself up, but he didn't have the strength to lift himself off the ground. Osmund grunted and walked over to him and picked him up with one hand before depositing him on Galine's back. Jez glared at him but said nothing.

Galine leapt forward, and Jez kept a death grip around the lion man's waist. The wind tore at him, and he had to shield his eyes. They moved through the trees so quickly that Jez saw only a green blur. He looked back, but his friends were nowhere in sight. He tried to call out to Galine, but his voice was drowned out by the wind.

After a few minutes, they stopped in the middle of a circle of trees near a narrow stream. Galine spent a while moving from tree to tree looking into branches, though Jez had no idea what he was looking for.

"Penar." Galine's voice bellowed over the sounds of the jungle, and birds chirped in response. "Penar, where are you?"

The trees rustled, and Galine turned in that direction. A few seconds later, Osmund and Lina came through, breathing heavily and drenched with sweat. Osmund gave Galine a level look as he wiped at his brow.

"You could've gone a little slower."

Galine huffed. "I went slow enough. You were able to find me, weren't you?"

"So where is this healer?"

Galine shrugged and extended his arms in a gesture that encompassed the surrounding trees. "This is his grove."

A brown streak drove out of the air. A rodent squealed as a hawk snatched it from the ground. It landed on a nearby branch and started tearing into its prey. Jez did a double take. It was only about a foot tall and underneath its wings, it had tiny arms which it used to

hold the dead rodent. Galine walked up to its tree and inclined his head.

"Penar."

The hawk screeched and flew to another tree, keeping a watch on Galine as it continued to eat. Galine raised an eyebrow at Lina. She nodded and reached up, but the branch was too high. She closed her eyes but opened them after a second and shook her head.

"I'm sorry. I need to be touching him."

"I'll get him," Osmund said.

"Don't hurt him," Galine said.

Osmund nodded and raised his hands. The hawk squawked as a gust of wind tore it from the branches. It spread its wings and tried to fly away, but another blast blew it down. It crashed into the ground, sinking a little into the muddy earth. Several feathers flew free. Galine growled.

"I said not to hurt him."

"Sorry, I don't exactly have fine control."

Lina grabbed the hawk as it tried to flap away. She cried out and Osmund moved over to her and held the animal's wings. Lina smiled at him for a second before closing her eyes. Once again, the violet mist poured out of her mouth and enveloped the hawk. It struggled for a few seconds before calming. Lina opened her eyes and nodded.

"Well, that was unexpected," the hawk said in precise words. He had an odd accent that reminded Jez of how Dusan had spoken. "Young man, would you mind letting me go?"

Osmund blinked and nodded, releasing the hawk's wings. It flapped up the tree and peered down at them. Its eyes focused on Galine.

"Galine, it's been a long time. Is that a human on your back? Goodness, he's hurt."

"It's why we came to you, Penar." Galine glared at Osmund before looking back to Penar. "Are you hurt?"

He ruffled his feathers. "Nothing serious. I've gotten worse than this from a particularly bad tempered falcon. Now, why don't I see to your injured friend, and you can tell me what's going on."

CHAPTER 43

Penar perched on Jez's shoulder. Orange light shone from between his feathers. Strength flowed into Jez as his blisters vanished. Penar couldn't heal the damage completely. It was a peculiarity of the transformation that the power hurt Jez in a way magic couldn't heal, but Penar could still return strength to him and help speed his body's natural healing abilities. After a few seconds, the hawk hopped off Jez shoulder and landed on the grass next to him.

"Well, that was more difficult than I thought it would be. I've never seen burns like that. What caused them?"

Jez shrugged. "It's complicated."

The hawk blinked at him. "Yes, I imagine it is." He turned to Galine who was seated nearby. "Now, would you mind telling me how I came under the influence of beast mind? I thought I'd moved past that long ago."

Penar's eyes couldn't widen, but he blinked several times as Galine related the relevant details. When he got to the part about Lina restoring his mind, Penar cooed at her and bowed. The motion looked so odd that Jez laughed, drawing the gazes of everyone there. He shrugged and nodded at Penar.

"An interesting story," the hawk said. "What help can I be?"

"This is worse than our ordinary internal bickering. I need you to intercede with Welb."

"I doubt he'd listen. He hates me even more than he hates you."

"Assuming he's even in his right mind," Galine said. "Even if he is, the others might be more reasonable. We'll gather without his consent if that's what we need to do."

Penar squawked and looked around the grove as if worried someone might overhear. When he spoke, it was in a soft voice that was nearly swallowed up by a breeze. "A splinter tribe? There hasn't been one of those in decades. It ended badly last time."

"I'd rather there be a war between tribes than have the whole of the Beastwalkers destroyed, and probably us along with them."

"Welb and the others may already be mad from what you say. How do you suggest I bring them out from under beast mind?"

Galine glanced at Lina but she wrinkled her brow. "Maybe your power can snap them out of it. It's not exactly beast mind."

"Close enough that I'll likely need mental magic to do anything for them." Galine started to speak, but Penar let out a soft caw. "No, you're right. It's worth a try. I'll do what I can. What will you do?"

"We need to find Aniel," Jez said.

"How?" Galine asked. "Last time, he found us."

"Last time, he wasn't under the influence of beast mind and rampaging through the jungle. I don't think he'll be that hard to find."

"Provided Sharim hasn't already done so."

"I don't think he has," Jez said. He motioned down at himself. "His body is no more able to bear transformation than mine is, and he was bitten by one of the snake men. He'll need time to recover."

"He could already be dead," Galine said. "You were in bad shape because of your transformation, and that venom is potent."

Jez shook his head. "There's no way we're that lucky. I assume you'll be able to find a destructive force of nature tearing through the jungle."

Galine stared at him for several seconds before inclining his head. "Just as soon as you're strong enough, I'll see if I can convince the bird men to help us."

Jez got to his feet, half expecting to feel weak as he so often had after healings, but he felt like he'd just had a full night's sleep. Even his injuries caused by transformation had been reduced to a dull pain. He looked at Penar.

"You're very good."

Penar bowed. "Human's focus too much on individual schools of magic. They're much more effective when you combine them. Healing together with beast can work wonders."

Jez blinked at the idea of combining schools of magic. It made sense, though he had never attempted it. Even so, the thought sent chills down his spine. Sharim had shown skills in at least three schools, and Jez suspected he'd only begun to see what the demon made flesh could do. He looked at Galine.

"Let's go."

CHAPTER 44

Galine knelt to examine a fallen tree. He pulled a tuft of black fur from a crack in the wood. The earth had been upturned, and the tree had been dragged twenty feet, seemingly by accident.

"He did this alone." Galine pointed down the path of destruction Aniel had made. "That way. He's much stronger than he should be as a hound, though I don't suppose that's terribly surprising, given who we're dealing with."

"He's heading for the lake," Jez said.

Galine nodded. "That makes sense."

"Why would a hound's mind lead him there?"

Galine snorted. "You really need to put away your prejudices. What we call the beast mind is not the mind of a beast overtaking the mind of its host. It's the improper mingling of two minds. A part of that creature is a hound, but another part is a high lord of the pharim, and Aniel's mind is stronger by far than any hound. It wouldn't be as completely overshadowed as a mortal's mind. The pharim in him likely senses the echoes of his own power."

Jez considered for a second before glancing at Lina. "Take Lina on your back."

"What?" Lina said.

"You're the only one who can restore Aniel's mind."

"Jez that won't work."

"It's worked twice before."

"On mortals. I've already tried to restore Aniel. His mind, if you can call it that, is just too alien."

Jez looked at her helplessly. "What are we going to do if we can't cure him?"

"Maybe we can capture him. At least that way we can keep him from falling into Sharim's hands."

"Capture him?" Galine asked. "You mean cage him. Cage a high lord of the pharim. How do you intend to do that?"

Lina's mouth dropped open a little, but she nodded and turned to Jez. "I think the catacombs under the Academy would work. When this whole thing started, you thought he might've been imprisoned there."

"You can't imprison Aniel," Galine said.

"Obviously not for long. Just long enough for Jez to contact..." She paused as she met Jez's gaze. Hiding who he was didn't serve a purpose anymore so he nodded. "The rest of the pharim."

Galine's chest rumbled, but if he'd been surprised by Lina's declaration, he didn't show it. "This isn't just any pharim. This is the lord of the Beastwalkers himself. You can't cage him."

"But—"

"Look," Jez cut in. "This is all a moot point unless we find him. Let's worry more about that and less about what to do when we do find him."

The trio nodded, and they started following the trail again. It didn't go directly for the lake. Rather, the path turned back on itself and wound through a circuitous route. A part of Jez wanted to just head to the lake, but he was worried they'd lose the trail. The animals were strangely silent, and according to Galine, there were far fewer than there usually were in this part of the jungle. They'd gone through half a dozen bends in the path before Jez caught the pattern.

In the middle of their trail was a hole, obviously dug by large paws. Water welled inside, and as soon as Jez touched it, he recognized the power of the lake. The prints of a massive hound showed that Aniel had stopped in front of the pool.

"I think he's drinking it." Jez turned to Galine. "Would that help restore him?"

"I don't have the slightest idea. It's not like this situation comes up very often."

"Haven't you ever drunk from the lake?"

Galine looked horrified. "No. Never." He held his hand over the water, though he didn't touch it. "For all intents and purposes, this is Aniel's blood. Even ordinary animals know better than to drink it, and no one with intelligence enough to know better would choose to drink."

"I didn't realize it was that special."

Galine narrowed his eyes. "It's the center of Aniel's power in this valley. Sharim used it to trap and then bind a pharim high lord. How could it not be special? It represents all he is, all the Beastwalkers are."

Jez nodded and sank his fingers into the water. Galine hissed but made no move to stop him. Jez closed his eyes and tried to meld his awareness with the water, hoping to find some hint of where Aniel was, but though he could sense the vast power in the water, he could draw no information from it. He was about to say as much when something brushed past his fingers. He pulled back and peered into the water to see a small fish swimming in circles. He withdrew his hand and looked up at Galine.

"I take it the water from the lake doesn't normally have fish in it."

Galine shook his head. "There's a river running through this valley that's fed by glacial runoff. There are fish and other animals living in that one, but on the streams fed by the lake? No."

"Well, there's something living here."

Galine blinked and walked up to the pool. He looked over Jez's shoulder. For a long time, he didn't say anything as the fish swam in a circle. When he finally did speak, his voice came out as a whisper.

"That's not possible."

"Lina, can you read its mind?"

Her jaw dropped a little, and she narrowed her eyes at him. "It's a fish."

"No, I don't think it is."

"What..." She glanced into the pool before meeting his eyes. "A Beastwalker?"

"Why else would Aniel have come here? I think he might be checking on them."

Lina shook her head. "Jez I already told you, I can't cure a Beastwalker's mind."

"You can tell a fish's mind from a pharim's, though."

"It's not that easy. They're so strange. It hurts my mind."

Jez rolled his eyes, and the crystal sword flickered into existence. He allowed himself to wince, and after a second, the weapon vanished. "Oh, if it's going to hurt, never mind. Goodness knows I always avoid things that are going to hurt."

She glared at him. "All right. You don't have to be so smug about it. I don't suppose you can catch it."

Jez let out a breath. He sank his hand slowly into the water and didn't move. Galine seemed to be trying not to speak, and after a few moments, he turned away. Osmund chuckled, and Jez grinned at him. For a few minutes, he kept his hand completely still. Something brushed against his fingertips, and his hand surged forward and closed around the fish. He withdrew his hand so quickly water splashed onto Lina's face. She cried out and when she was done wiping her face, he held the flopping fish in his hand.

"Where did you learn to do that?"

Jez grinned. "I'm the son of a fisherman, remember. I've spent hours with fish catching them every way there is." He held the animal out to her. "You should hurry. If this really is a Beastwalker, I wouldn't want to suffocate it."

She reached out slowly and touched it. It flopped and she pulled back. Jez let out a breath and rolled his eyes. He lifted his hand toward her face. "They can't survive very long outside of water. You really should hurry."

"Sorry," she said and she touched it again. She let out a small squeal but closed her eyes. After a second she opened it again. "It's a Beastwalker. I don't know how to fix its mind, but it definitely is one of them."

Jez nodded and slipped the fish back into the water. He pursed his lips. "Sharim was able to force me to transform."

Galine nodded. "Yes, but he had tapped into Aniel's power."

Jez touched the water's surface with the tip of his finger. "Isn't that what this is?"

"But will restoring its body restore its mind?"

"It might," Jez said. "A pharim's form is essentially whatever they see themselves as. If I can force this Beastwalker back into a humanoid shape, it might force his mind to revert too."

Lina looked uncertain. "Jez, you never studied transformation magic. Are you sure you want to try this?"

"I'm sure we could use a pharim by our side."

"You could hurt him," Galine said.

"Right now, a hungry bird could hurt him."

Galine looked to the sky. His eyes locked on a sparrow that was flitting from branch to branch. The bird didn't look to be coming in their direction, but it was still big enough to take a bite out of the Beastwalker. Galine nodded.

"You're right. Do it."

CHAPTER 45

Once again, Jez sank his power into the water. It resisted him, but with his hands actually inside the pool, he was able to push past it with a little effort. Still, it was like trying to hold onto an eel. If the Beastwalker hadn't actually been in the water less than a foot from Jez's hand, he would've never been able to find it. Its swimming was erratic as if it could feel Jez's presence in the water and feared it. Jez surrounded it with his power. It swam deeper, trying to escape, but instinctively, Jez directed the transformation power and seized the pharim.

Its form was wrong. This Beastwalker was a radiant spirit that had existed since the beginning of time, and now, it had been forced into a body ill-suited to contain its brilliance. Its power rebelled against its form, but that same form was too strong, bolstered by a working he didn't understand.

Jez tried to direct the transformation power flowing through him, but it was like trying to redirect a river by standing in it. He thought back to Penar's words about combining schools of magic. Without being sure exactly how he did it, he melded his aqua magic with the transformation power instilled in the water. Using the ability he was most skilled at, he shaped the power in the water, focusing it into a

sharp point. He stabbed at the magic holding the pharim's form in place, and the shell of the working cracked. Green mist spilled into the water as the fish melted away. Aniel's power was torn from Jez's grasp as water exploded out of the pool. When it had settled, a creature that was as much fish as man stood before them.

It was covered from head to toe in shimmering scales that went from white on its chest and stomach to silver around its head. Its hands and feet were webbed and fins sprouted from its forearms. It had gill slits on its neck, and sea-green eyes were set wide on a face that was longer than it was tall. Its wings were covered in scales and gave the impression that they were better suited to swimming than flying, though Jez had no doubt the pharim could accomplish either. Like the other Beastwalkers Jez had seen, it wore a sword at its waist that looked more like a long claw or horn than a blade of worked steel. Its edge was serrated, and Jez found himself reminded of the teeth of a shark.

"My lord Beastwalker?" Galine said.

The fish man blinked at him and turned to look back at the pool. His exit had emptied it of most of the water, though it was slowly filling again, presumably fed by some underground spring. He stared at the rising water before sighing at Jez.

"What's wrong with him?" Galine asked.

"I think it's the same thing that was wrong with Aniel. He's not insane with anger anymore, but his mind hasn't recovered."

"Then, this accomplished nothing."

"I don't know about that," Jez said. He stepped up to the Beastwalker. "Aniel. Do you know Aniel?"

The pharim stood up to his full height of nearly seven feet. He looked into the distance and stared for several seconds, completely unmoving. Then he blinked at Jez and started running. For a moment, Jez and the others just looked at each other. Then, they took off.

Though Galine was obviously trying to run as fast as he could, they kept up with him. The pharim never got very far ahead of them, never disappearing from sight for more than a second or two. It seemed impossible that anything with webbed feet like that could move so fast, but the jungle may as well have been water for all it impeded the Beastwalker. The forest blurred, and Jez found himself feeling light on his feet. He knew he should be out of breath by now, but the run hadn't tired him at all. He wasn't even making any special effort to avoid obstructions. He just ran on.

He was having trouble keeping his thoughts in line. All he could think about was the run. One step at a time. He just needed to do one step at a time. He knew he'd started with companions, but he had no idea where they had gone to. All that existed to him was the Beastwalker running through the mist ahead of him. Suddenly, it leapt ten feet into the air, sailing over a boulder and splashing into the river on the other side. Jez and his companions stopped at the shore and exchanged glances. A quick examination of the river revealed it was fed by Aniel's lake. Though the water was clear, there were no fish at all, and they saw no sign of the pharim.

"Well that was...odd," Osmund said.

"He's probably going back to the lake. Either he detected Aniel there or..."

Galine cut it. "Or he was still more fish than pharim. This was a waste of time. Let's head back to Aniel's trail." He blinked and looked around. "Huh."

"What is it?" Jez asked.

"We're in a completely different area of the valley. We've gone at least five miles."

"That's not possible," Jez said. "I mean we were only running a few minutes. Maybe you could cover that distance..."

Galine shook his head. "Not even on the open plains with the wind at my back."

Jez thought back to their run. "Did you see the mist too?"

Lina's mouth opened a little and she nodded. "I didn't notice it before, but looking back, yes." She looked around. "There's no mist though."

"He took us Between." Osmund nodded, but Lina and Galine looked confused. Jez shook his head. "It would take too long to explain. Basically it's how pharim can get from place to place quickly. I don't think we were in there all the way though. We were partially still in the jungle."

"I didn't know they could do that," Osmund said.

"Neither did I." He turned to Galine. "Where exactly are we?"

"About a mile from the western shore of Aniel's lake."

"And about a hundred yards from my camp," Welb said as he stepped out of the trees. He focused on Jez and showed his teeth. "I seem to recall exiling you for bringing this disaster on us. Give me one reason I shouldn't rip your throat out."

CHAPTER 46

Galine stepped in front of Jez. "How many do you have with you, Welb? How many are still sane?"

Welb growled. "I have enough."

"They drove you out of town, didn't they?"

Welb's muscles tensed and for a second, it looked like he was about to jump at Galine. Instead, he snarled.

"Was that your fault too?"

"It was the fault of the creature that has invaded our valley. Maybe if you weren't so caught up in your hatred of humans, we might have been able to stop him."

"He is a human!"

"He's no more human than any of the tribe, and quite a bit less than most." Galine narrowed his eyes. "Except you, of course. You alone, of all of us, lack even a shred of humanity."

"Your humanity makes you weak. Look what has resulted."

Welb's voice was a barely controlled rage, and Jez half expected to see him foaming at the mouth, but Galine remained completely calm.

"When did Aniel demand that we rid ourselves of it?" he asked. "Isn't the purpose of this place to find a balance between the natures the beast and the man?"

"That nature of man has led to this."

"No," Jez said. "Sharim was a demon from birth. Human nature had no part in this."

"Listen to him, Welb," Penar said as he landed on a nearby branch.

"You're even worse than he is. At least he gave up most of his human power."

"And yet it's that human power that has given you what warriors you have. If you so disdain its use, you are free to face this Sharim on your own."

"You have no right to oppose me," Welb said. "I have won the right of challenge."

"The right of challenge only applies to those who have chosen to live in the town." The hawk gave him a piercing glare. "To those who have a more human existence." Welb curled back his lips and gnashed his teeth, but Penar continued. "The town is gone, and your authority ended with it. Even if it had not, I never made my home there."

Welb snarled in Galine's direction. "He led us to destruction."

"If not for his human friends, he would still be mad and so would I. You would be alone."

"I will not follow him into battle," Welb said, staring at Galine.

"Then follow me," Jez said as he stepped around Galine and looked up at Welb.

The wolf man glared down at him. His jaw dropped, and he looked from Galine to Penar and back to Jez. Jez felt the need to back up, but restrained himself and didn't turn from Welb's gaze.

"You can't be serious."

"The others will follow him," Penar said.

"A human?"

"A human that I'll follow," Galine said.

"As will I," Penar said. "Oppose him if you wish, but you will do so without my support, and likely without the support of those I have restored."

Welb glared up into the trees for a minute before storming off into the jungle.

"So you were able to restore them?" Jez asked once Welb was gone.

Penar ruffled his feathers, as gesture that Jez was coming to recognize as about equal to shaking your head. "Only a few, and those likely would've come out of it in a few days anyway."

"How many are there?"

"Six, not counting Welb."

"Only six?"

Penar's glare almost seemed to look right through Jez. "Shall we go and investigate your troops?"

CHAPTER 47

To Jez's surprise, Grita was one of those Penar had healed. Even more surprising was the nod of respect she gave Jez. All of the beast men were closer to being humans than animals. The farthest from that was a turtle woman whose shell made her look like an animal that had decided to walk upright. She had a curved beak that reminded Jez of the snapping turtles that he'd sometimes found on the shores of the river near Randak. It would probably be dangerous in a fight. In fact, all of them seemed well suited to combat.

"It's not that surprising when you think of it," Penar said when Jez asked.

"It's not?"

Penar ruffled his feathers. "I don't have your friend's gift for restoring the mind, and I could only help those closest to being human. War has always been a human failing. Naturally, any I restore are likely to have an aspect of that in their personality, and their forms reflect that."

"I guess that makes sense," Jez said, though he only half understood what Penar meant. "Still this isn't much of an army." Osmund smirked, and Jez glared at him. "What?"

"I'm pretty sure that's exactly what you said that time we fought off an army of demons. That didn't turn out too badly."

Jez raised an eyebrow. "You know, the last I heard, Haziel was still repairing the front gate of his castle from when that demon burst through it."

Osmund shrugged. "I mean it didn't turn out too badly for us. We all walked out of there, didn't we?"

Jez looked Osmund in the eye for several seconds before the mirth on the other boy faded. Eventually, Osmund took several steps back and inclined his head. "Ok, I guess that was a little difficult wasn't it?"

Jez shook his head. "You're hopeless. Let's head to Aniel's lake. Keep an eye out for any other beast men. Lina should be able to help them."

There were nods all around and they started walking. The jungle seemed silent as they moved through it, as if the trees themselves were holding their breath and waiting to see what would happen. Jez sank his power into the earth and found the water flowing beneath. This close to the lake, the ground was soaked. It practically hummed with power, even more than he'd felt in Aniel's presence.

"They're in there," Jez said. The others looked at him and he gestured in the direction they were going. "I think the pharim are all in the lake. The water feels practically alive."

"Do you think Sharim knows?" Galine asked.

"He will as soon as he tries to tap into the lake's power." Jez's eyes went wide. "Oh no."

"What is it?" Galine asked.

"Are we anywhere near the circle we found on the lake shore?"

"It's just over that rise. Why?"

"Sharim's going to use it."

"You destroyed it."

Jez shook his head. "I disabled it."

Galine grabbed him by the shoulders. "Are you telling me he can repair it?"

"No, but it's like rowing a leaky boat. If you row fast enough, you can still get where you're going before it sinks. Sharim's going to pour enough power into it that what I did won't matter."

"You knew this was a possibility?"

Jez tore away from him. "Did I know it was possible to use a disabled circle if you pour enough power into it? Yes. Did I know Sharim would have access to the power of the lake amplified a thousand times because of the presence of every Beastwalker in existence?" Jez shook his head. "He would've never been able to do it with anything less."

Galine stared at him for a few seconds before looking into the distance. He made a curt gesture with his hand and bounded into the trees. The other beast men ran forward. Jez rushed after him, Osmund and Lina running right behind him.

CHAPTER 48

They came out of the tree line and looked out onto the land before them. The lake shimmered in the distance. The runes of the circle at its edge shone so brightly they left an afterimage in Jez's vision. He could barely make out Sharim standing at the edge with arms raised. Dark shapes swirling around him stood as a sharp contrast to the light of the circle. Jez thought he caught a faint whiff of sulfur, but at that distance, it was impossible to be sure. Still, he didn't really need it to tell what was going on.

"He's summoning demons," he said to Galine. "It could be to possess animals or to possess you."

A shadow passed over them, and Jez looked up to see a bright red bird circling and coming in for a landing. It landed on Jez's shoulder. Though its body was red, the long feathers on its wings were bright blue with a few green feathers separating them from the red. The tail was a mix of blue and red, and it had flaps of white skin around its eyes. It had a curved beak that Jez suspected was good for cracking open nuts. It watched a large lizard sunning on a nearby rock before hopping closer to Jez's ear.

"Saw you." The bird let out a low whistle. "We attack from south. Coordinate."

The bird whistled again before taking off to the south. Jez stared at it until it vanished into the trees. He turned to Galine.

"Was that a beast man?"

"Just a parrot." When he saw the confused look on Jez's face he went on. "It's a type of bird that can learn to imitate human speech. I've never seen one used as a messenger before. It takes too long to train them for it to be feasible."

"What about with beast magic?"

Galine nodded. "It's possible, though it's a rather frivolous use of the power."

Lina chuckled. "My entire school of magic is rather frivolous. It's not surprising that others have those kinds of uses too."

"You don't understand. The beast mind is a crucible that burns away all the excess and leaves only the core of a personality behind."

Lina smirked. "I've met frivolous people before. Trust me, the nobility is full of them."

"And how many of them are mages of any real skill?"

Lina's smile vanished. "Not many. Actually, none. There are a few mages that pretend to be like the other nobles, but it's all an act to gain political power."

"Frivolous personalities don't make it far as mages, certainly not far enough to transform and stay that way for weeks on end."

The darkness around Sharim moved faster, shading him entirely. Then, as if flung by some great force, a piece of the darkness flew into the jungle. One by one, other shades did the same, pelting the jungle with shadow. One flew in the direction of Jez and his companions. Jez fell back, barely managing to avoid screaming. It hit the lizard. The animal hissed and started to grow. Jez reacted without thinking, moving his hand from the creature's head to its heart. Inky blackness billowed from its nose and mouth. It started to solidify, but

Osmund threw a ball of fire, and the darkness disappeared in a puff of smoke. The lizard scurried into the bushes before the flames had even started to fade.

The jungle erupted in howls and roars as the lotheen took control of their prey. The trees to the south rustled. Welb charged out, his claw blade emitting brilliant green light. Lacking the support of beast men, Welb had found other allies. Behind him came wolves, lions, and every type of animal who lived in the valley. They were heading right for Sharim. Without waiting for a command from Jez, the beast men charged Sharim as well.

CHAPTER 49

At least fifty creatures thundered behind Welb, and the beast men joined his forces before they had gone a quarter of the way. Sharim looked at them, utter contempt showing on his face. He lifted a hand and the green crystal at his feet flared to life. The animals froze in their tracks, all but Welb, who kept running.

A wave of shadows washed over the clearing toward the animals. Welb held his sword before him as if to catch the shadows. It glowed, forming a pillar of green light. Jez had spent nearly a year studying demons. Protection magic could guard against them and destruction magic could banish them, but there was no way beast magic could have any effect on them. Jez stopped in his tracks as the shadows fell upon Welb.

And they turned aside.

They split on the sword, half going to either side and missing the animals entirely. For a second, Sharim just stared, his mouth open in shock. Welb raised his sword and as his light fell upon the animals, they began to move again. A lion let out a roar, and the animals surged forward like a wave. Then, the jungle cried out.

Disfigured animals, far larger than their counterparts, rushed out of the trees. Even Welb stopped and stared. The possessed animals ran toward the natural creatures with Welb. The afur backed up until he stood in the middle of the creatures. At first, Jez thought he was hiding, but as the light intensified, he realized he was wrong. The natural animals didn't grow or become more muscular, but they suddenly stood straighter, with muscles tensed. They just seemed like more than they had been.

"He's making them stronger," Jez said.

There were more of the demonic animals than the normal ones, but enhanced by Welb's power, that seemed not to matter. The animals on both sides moved with deadly speed, but Sharim's beasts seemed just a little slower. Their teeth always missed by inches and their claws never seemed to catch anything but fur or feathers.

"Reminds you a little of Rumar, doesn't it?" Osmund said. "When the townspeople distracted the demon so we could assault the castle." His form rippled, and Ziary stood before him. The scion pointed his flaming sword at Sharim. His eyes blazed. "The way is open."

Jez looked to Sharim who was engrossed with his ritual to call up more demons. Now that they were closer, he could see the snake-like scales covering Sharim. His hair had fallen out, and his arm looked frail and withered. He'd obviously used transformation magic to deal with the poison, but it hadn't come without a price. Jez nodded, and Galine came to stand next to him.

"I'll hide your approach," Lina said, "and I'll do whatever else I can from here."

"Don't get ahead of me," Jez said. "He probably has that shield around him, and I want to be close enough that he won't have time to react when I take it down."

Galine and Ziary nodded and after a few seconds, the world dimmed as Lina hid them from sight. They charged toward Sharim. As they got within a few yards, Jez's fingers wove a complex pattern.

The barrier flashed into sight then shattered. Sharim's eyes went wide as they attacked.

CHAPTER 50

Sharim bent backward at an impossible angle as both Jez's and Ziary's blades sliced the air above him. Galine's heavy paw slammed into Sharim's side, sending him to the ground. Jez followed up with a thrust, but Sharim moved like lightning, twisting out of the way without bothering to stand, and Jez's sword sank into the earth, cutting into the edge of the circle. Jez screamed as transformation magic travelled up his blade and spilled into his body.

He could feel everything. Ziary and Galine fought nearby, transformation power filling them. At a distance, the energy Welb fed into the creatures around him glowed like a beacon. The lotheen in the animals reflected a dark transformation of their own, and on the other side of Jez, the lake practically sang with power. The part of him that was Luntayary stirred and came to the surface. Jez couldn't tell which pain was greater, that of the pharim within burning away his flesh or the nearly boundless transformation energy coursing through his body.

Jez tried to push Luntayary back, and for a moment, he thought he would succeed, but nearby, Sharim laughed, a hissing sound that would've made Jez shiver if he hadn't been overcome by pain. Luntayary lumbered forward, slow but unstoppable. He came even more fully than before, and Jez knew he had mere seconds before the Shadowguard overwhelmed him.

"Ziary."

Jez wasn't sure if he'd spoken the word or just thought it. Ziary was a scion of the pharim. Luntayary was more powerful by far, but they were the same type of being. Osmund was a descendent of the afur, beings like Welb, the pharim who had rebelled. He was not entirely human and so his body could bear the transformation Ziary brought on him. Jez could feel the difference in Osmund's flesh even as it was being suppressed by Ziary. Perhaps if he could copy it...

He grabbed the transformation power flowing through him and directed it at himself. Even as Luntayary's power burned his flesh, Aniel's power changed it. He would never be able to contain the fullness of Luntayary's power. It was simply beyond the capacity of mortal flesh, but he could make his body better able to bear it.

The pain receded. It still hurt enough to make him want to cry out, but it was no longer the incapacitating agony that had prevented him from acting. The world became clear, and he realized his wings had emerged and his clothes had been transformed to sapphire robes. His sword still buzzed with the transformation energy he'd absorbed from the circle. He rose and looked around.

Welb, Ziary, and Galine, as well as the rest of the beast men, had been bound by strange bands of green energy. Ziary's robes were torn, and Galine had several burn marks on his chest. The next instant, pain ran through Jez's body, but it was little more than a pinprick next to what he'd felt a moment ago, and he shrugged it off. He turned to Sharim who had his left arm extended toward Jez. In his right, he held a sword of liquid flame. Jez took a shaky step toward him, and the pain intensified. It was like fire burning throughout his body, but he kept his head up and took another step.

"That's impossible."

Jez was gasping, but he managed to force out the words. "Impossible." He took several breaths. "I'm surprised you would use that word Sharim, given what you are."

Sharim's smile showed curved teeth that dripped with venom. "It's impressive that you're able to control yourself, but you can barely stand."

Sharim delivered a quick slash with his sword, and it was all Jez could do to raise his own weapon. The same weapon that still hummed with the power of transformation. If Sharim had been using an ordinary blade, there would've been little Jez could do, but Sharim wielded the weapon of a demon, and it was as much a part of Sharim as Jez's sword was a part of him. It was alive, and beast magic was the magic of things that were alive.

The liquid flame died and solidified into a sword that looked like it was made of orange glass. Sharim grunted and tried to relight it, but Jez's power held. Sharim scowled and threw his sword aside. It puffed into smoke before it hit the ground.

"I don't need this to defeat you. You're good with that borrowed power, but you're not practiced."

Sharim held both his hands toward Jez and the power that had been coursing through him was torn from his grasp. Sharim directed the power at the lake, and the waters started to churn. There was a deafening roar as a serpent larger than any Jez had ever imagined rose from the water. Its emerald scales shimmered in the sunlight. Its body was at least as wide as Jez was tall and its serpentine head was fifty feet above the water. It roared, showing razor sharp teeth. Such a creature was too big to inhabit that lake. Sharim had to have transformed it, and Jez had a cold certainty he knew what this thing

had been before, and if he was right, he couldn't allow himself to kill it.

"Aniel," Sharim shouted. "Kill him."

CHAPTER 51

Jez forced Luntayary back until the pain from the pharim's overwhelming power no longer inhibited him. The serpent lunged at him, but he spread his wings and flew above Aniel's attack. The pharim lord turned upward, its brilliant green eyes focusing on Jez. It tried to bite again, and Jez delivered a quick slash to its nose, spilling motes of glowing green energy. For a moment, confusion flashed across Aniel's face, but it was replaced by rage a moment later as the serpent reared its head and roared.

"What kind of creature are you?" Jez asked under his breath. Aniel snapped again. This time, he caught a piece of Jez's robe, and it tore off.

Jez sank his power into the water and tried to ensnare Aniel's form, but as a tendril wrapped around the great serpent, the water recognized its master and struck back at Jez. Pain blossomed in his head, and the next thing he knew, he was falling. The surface of the water rushed toward him.

Jez tried to flap, but his wings had vanished. He screamed, and something erupted from the water. Strong arms caught him. Jez blinked and realized it was the fish-like pharim from before. They landed on the shore. Aniel roared, but in the next instant, the air around him was filled with birds and the waters near him churned with fish. Strands of green energy shot out of an eagle flying around Aniel's head. They connected with other birds who spawned green strands of their own. The energy spread out among the animals, eventually joining with the fish and forming a net. The animals closed in on Aniel, wrapping him in energy.

"Those are all pharim, aren't they?" Jez asked. "They're all Beastwalkers. You called them."

The fish man put Jez on the ground. It smiled before spreading its fin-like wings and taking to the air. A wave of heat washed over Jez and he turned to see Sharim rushing toward him, his flaming sword once again in his hand. Jez raised his hand. His sword popped into existence at the last second. The two blades clashed together with a sound like thunder.

"You've only delayed your own demise. Even all the Beastwalkers together can't long restrain Aniel."

The focusing crystal in Sharim's hand glowed, and behind Jez, Aniel roared. Jez tried to take the power from Sharim, but either Sharim was too powerful or his experience was too great. The transformation energy slipped through Jez's fingers.

Sharim laughed. Again and again Sharim struck. He attacked with a casual ease that Jez, in his weakened state, couldn't counter. Sharim delivered a hard blow. Jez caught it on his sword, but the force of the impact sent him to the ground. Sharim put his sword at Jez's neck. Its flames sent agony surging through Jez's body, but Sharim didn't press it in. Instead, he laughed.

"You made a good show of it, but you never really stood a chance."

He looked at the lake behind Jez. Jez risked a glance over his shoulder. The green energy net had tightened around Aniel, but the pharim lord let out a roar, and the energy exploded outward as the pharim were thrown away. Aniel cut through the water, heading right toward Jez. Again, Jez tried to seize the transformation power from Sharim, but it was no use. The focusing crystal made his control too absolute.

With Jez's body weakened from his transformation, and Sharim ahead and Aniel behind, Jez was out of options. He drew deeply of Luntayary's power. Sharim's sword pressed a little harder, and Jez knew he wouldn't be able to move before his foe skewered him. Jez clenched his teeth and drew even deeper.

Though his sword was a potent weapon, it was not his only one. He was a Shadowguard. He knew protection magic. He might not be skilled but he was still strong. Protection magic was the magic of warding and binding. The magic of water, and it was the magic of earth. The power burned in him. He wouldn't be able to last long, but he wouldn't last long without it either. He directed all of his power at the focusing crystal. Aniel had created it from his own will, but in changing it, he had made it into a crystal, and crystals were made of earth.

It shattered in an explosion of green energy. A wave of power washed over Jez, banishing Luntayary's form. Sharim too returned to normal. As the energy hit Aniel, it twisted around him, encircling him. He threw back his head, but the cry that came out sounding more human than anything else Jez had heard from the pharim lord. The form of the great serpent melted away leaving the antlered form of Aniel suspended in the air. Aniel's eyes locked onto the shore, and with only a few flaps of his great wings, he landed next to Jez. He drew his claw blade and advanced toward Sharim.

"No," Sharim said, panic painting his face. "I am human. You cannot interfere."

Aniel took another step forward. The jungle erupted in animal cries, but somehow, Aniel's quiet voice could be heard over it.

"Not unless you interfere with me."

Sharim paled and backed up several steps. He seemed to be moving faster than Aniel, but for some reason, the gap between them continued to shrink until Aniel stood before him. Sharim grasped at his chest. A thin chain around his neck that Jez hadn't noticed before snapped, and Sharim pulled out what seemed to be an obsidian crystal. Rather than glow, it shed darkness.

Aniel's eyes shone as he raised his sword, point down. He drove it toward Sharim, but the shadows coalesced beneath Sharim. A hole opened, and he fell into a circle of blackness. It closed and Aniel's blade stabbed into the earth. A bright aura of green light surrounded Aniel, and his face twisted in anger.

"What happened?" Jez asked.

"He's fled into the abyss."

CHAPTER 52

With the crystal gone, there was nothing keeping the Beastwalkers from returning the core of their power to the Keep of the Hosts. Then, they spread out through the valley, restoring the minds of both the beast men and the animals that had been affected by Sharim. Penar did what he could to heal Jez's wounds, but too much magic had gone through his body recently, and he needed rest almost as much as he needed healing. Galine carried him back to the remnants of the village. Though the fires were out, it seemed like nothing more than a collection of burned out husks.

"What will you do?" Jez asked.

"Rebuild, eventually," Galine said. "We are not so soft that we actually need to live in buildings. Perhaps Welb had a point."

"What happened to him?" Jez asked. "I didn't see him after the battle."

"Perhaps he wanted to avoid confronting Aniel."

"I did," Welb said as he came out of the trees. Some of the beast men came after him. "You've seen me, though. So have many others, and I'm not so arrogant as to believe I can hide from a high lord of the pharim who has decided to look for me."

There was a laugh that seemed to come from everywhere at once. Lizards swarmed in front of Welb, and what had to be a hundred flying insects landed on top of them. The animals swirled together before resolving into the form of Aniel. The beast men gasped and took a step back. Welb started to shake but controlled himself after a second. Aniel smiled.

"Did you think you had hidden from me before?"

Welb blinked at him. "You knew?"

Aniel inclined his head. "You are no longer a Beastwalker, and you did not claim to be."

"I was afraid you would be angry."

"Your punishment was given when you were cast from the Keep of the Hosts. I want nothing more from you. If you wish to live among the beast men, I have no objection."

"Thank you, Lord Aniel."

The high lord of the Beastwalkers nodded once. Then, his form exploded into a cloud of insects, all of which flew in a different direction.

"But what about Sharim," Osmund asked once Aniel had gone. "What's to stop him from coming back?"

"He can't," Jez said. Osmund looked at him. "Do you remember what Villia said when I was going to follow Shamarion into the abyss? You can't go into the abyss of your own free will and come out again the same way. He's gone."

"Unless he's summoned," Lina said.

"What do you mean?"

She wrinkled her nose at him. "Jez, six month ago, Sharim tried to summon an army at Rumar. Today, he tried to summon one here. Are you sure he didn't succeed sometime between then and now?"

"Are you saying there could be a demon army out there?"

She nodded. "One that might have the ability to summon him back."

"If he comes back here," Grita said as she walked up next to Welb, "we'll be ready."

"You're not coming back?" Jez asked.

She shook her head and looked over her shoulder at Toden who was helping to clear away some of the rubble to make way for new houses. "It was real beast mind that took us. It might have been brought on by Aniel's condition, but that doesn't make it false. We can't go back."

"Maybe if I spoke to Horgar," Jez started.

She shook her head. "Our place is here. We'll guard it and leave the rest of the world to you."

"I'm staying too," Osmund said.

"What?"

Osmund raised a hand. "Not forever. Just long enough to see if I can find some balance with me and Ziary. I have a feeling we'll need it."

Jez thought about that for a second. He'd started to hope this was all over, but deep down, he'd known it was a fantasy. Sharim would not have fled into the abyss without a plan to escape. Whether demonic or human, Sharim had allies. This wasn't over, but for today, at least, they had won.

ABOUT THE AUTHOR

Gama Ray Martinez lives near Salt Lake City, Utah. He moved there solely because he likes mountains. He collects weapons in case he ever needs to supply a medieval battalion, and he greatly resents when work or other real life things get in the way of writing. He secretly hopes to one day slay a dragon in single combat and doesn't believe in letting pesky things like reality get in the way of his dreams. Find him at http://gamarayburst.com/ and http://www.facebook.com/gamarayburst

www.ingramcontent.com/pod-product-compliance
Lightning Source LLC
Chambersburg PA
CBHW050349190726
48284CB00007BB/2214